AFTER IT HAPPENED

BOOK 5: SANCTUARY

DEVON C FORD

Originally self-published by Devon C Ford in 2016

Published by Vulpine Press in the United Kingdom in 2017

ISBN: 978-1-83919-228-9

www.vulpine-press.com

Dedicated to my mini-mes, who want to sleep in every day except weekends.

PROLOGUE

Bullets whined, fizzed and screamed past them. Ricochets pinged through a seemingly impossible spectrum of sound, punctuated by shouts and screams. The percussive coughs of return fire through their suppressed weapons sounded like a woefully inadequate response to the maelstrom of noise and lead being sent towards them, but deep under the stress lay the knowledge that the end result of receiving a bullet from either side would be the same.

Conducting a fighting withdrawal with a platoon of trained men would have been difficult; scrambling away to safety with a handful of half-trained men, women and children while under fire was another thing entirely.

They were leaderless, they were scared, and they had lost.

All of these facts Mitch blamed himself for. In a matter of minutes, he had become the thing he despised most in a solider: inefficient.

A thought ran through his head, moving far quicker than the bullets singing through the air around them.

The speed of thought, somewhere between the swiftness of sound and light, he reckoned. Certainly faster than the muzzle velocities of the weapons aimed at them.

Fast enough to consider the stupidity and desperation of the situation they had stumbled into.

Fast enough to understand that they weren't under attack from trained men, or the accuracy of their shots would have claimed more victims by now.

Fast enough to know that when the adrenaline wore off, his chest would likely be badly bruised by the bullet which had slammed violently into his ballistic vest and knocked him on his face.

Fast enough to consider their best option: run.

Run fast and get out of the line of fire.

FLEETING HAPPINESS

From behind the wheel of his monstrous new ride, Dan's mind wandered happily. This was his second autumn since the world died and began its slow process of decaying, but he had thrived and now felt more alive than before.

He had met Neil and the two had come up with a plan to start a new life for everyone they could save. Dan had rescued a young, frightened girl first, who was now sitting beside him dressed like a warrior. A smile crept onto his face as he thought that the girl picking a speck of dust from the breech of her rifle had transformed from frightened to frightening.

Their numbers swelled until they experienced their first brush with the hostility of other people. It still worried Dan how simple a thing it was to take a life when it was justified by an "us or them" concept.

Their life at the prison had grown almost comfortable; running water and a hot shower was something he could only dream of now, let alone a sustainable power supply.

When he had met Marie, his life changed again. The passing of Penny and the internal struggles they fought were nothing compared to the suffering of others. As those more unfortunate were liberated by Dan's ever-increasing thirst for justice, they had formed a home to be proud of.

Others had come for them, and they had lost. Dan felt guilty about leaving their home to chase the rainbow of a solution to the tragic problems facing anyone who fell pregnant, and that guilt was amplified when so many chose to follow him. His home, their home, seemed so far away now.

He comforted himself in knowing that he had left them under the very capable leadership of the former Royal Air Force pilot, but he had no way to know that Steve had been horribly injured in a helicopter crash.

If he knew that their home was gone, eradicated in a single blow, and his people taken under the dubious protection of a man he would happily kill with his bare hands, then his guilt would overcome him in an instant. If he knew that his first protégé, Lexi, was on the run and having to rely on the skills he had taught her, he would probably consider throwing a U-turn and heading back.

But he knew nothing of the terrible events at home. For now, his whole world was in the four military vehicles driving in convoy across Germany. They were fantastically well equipped, ridiculously well supplied with food and fuel, and they were heading to a place far away for possible answers.

The lunacy of their plan had struck him more than once since they had left, crossed the English Channel in unseasonably bad weather and wound their ponderous way across Europe, making yet more friends in the way he usually did.

Flexing his hands on the chunky steering wheel of his new ride with a glance in the side mirrors to see the convoy proudly following, he had to admit that he was having a good day so far.

THE LEXI ROADSHOW

Their fuel ran out an hour before daylight, and without the tools they normally carried, they couldn't find any to continue their journey in the stolen vehicle.

Fearful of pursuit ever since they fled their home and murdered two of the attackers, they rolled the car off the road into some bushes where the natural slope hid it from any casual observer. The gap it left in the foliage was obvious enough to Lexi, but she didn't think it would help her standing among the other three to sound negative right now.

She was fairly certain that Chris and Melissa hated her, and even Paul's love for her couldn't be totally relied on right then. She blamed herself for the attack on their home, and like everyone wallowing in self-pity, she was convinced that the others held the same opinion. It was time to step up and prove herself worthy of leading the last remnants of the society they used to feel secure in.

In truth, they did hold her responsible for the way things turned out, at least to some extent. If she hadn't acted childishly, then her objections to the twins' appointment may have been listened to instead of everyone dismissing her opinion as a continuation of her bad attitude.

She wanted to explain that it wasn't fair. She had raised legitimate concerns which were ignored, and she couldn't be held responsible for the actions of others. She knew it was a weak argument, and it was still a very raw subject, having fled with next to nothing only hours before.

The dried blood of the man she had killed caked her clothes from neck to knee, and both of her hands looked black in the low light of the pre-dawn. At least her black clothing hid the worst of the stains.

Without maps, they were forced to take direction from the rising sun and place it on their left as they walked. They were in an area that she had not scouted over the last year or so, and they moved cautiously as a result. Just like Dan had taught her, she put herself up front, placed Paul at the back as a rearguard and protected the two most vulnerable in the middle as they walked along in single file. Both Chris and Melissa were carrying the weapons taken from the two dead sentries, but the guns themselves were as untested as the people carrying them.

She had to rely on what they had, which wasn't much, and make their situation better. Shelter, supplies, transport. In that order. They had unanimously agreed the plan as they moved through the dark: get to Africa and find the others.

As a plan it was simple, but the moving parts of that plan were numerous and complex.

What if they couldn't find a car? They were weeks away from walking to the south coast if they had to move in slow fear.

What if they couldn't find a boat? Could they get through the tunnel?

What if they met any hostility? They were unlikely to have any chance against similar or superior numbers, so they would have to rely on stealth.

The feeling of being hunted made for a heightened state of anxiety in all of them, so she fell back once more to Dan's instruction: hide during the day and move at night; it was slower but safer. But that only made sense if she was on foot, as driving at night attracted far more attention than in the day. *Damn him*, she thought, *why did he have to leave?* Why didn't she learn more from him and Steve instead of strutting around with her newly acquired status?

She shook those thoughts away, as she had to make a decision: stop for the day and continue that night or find a vehicle? Follow Dan's word like the gospel or make her own path?

She called a stop as the other three huddled in towards her, stressed and exhausted. Taking a knee and fiddling with her rifle to gain a few valuable seconds of thinking time, just as Dan did, she told the others what she wanted.

"We need a vehicle," she said firmly.

Looks of relief washed over all of them, telling her that she had already gone some small way to repairing their trust in her. Giving people what they needed instead of what they wanted was often an unpopular way to go, but giving them what they wanted and not what they needed was bound to result in failure.

Failure meant capture, or death by any number of means. She could not fail.

"We'll move towards the town over there," she went on, pointing to the tops of buildings in the distance, "and you two will hole up somewhere while we find what we need."

Melissa especially seemed relieved to be given a role where she no longer had to walk. Paul remained tight-lipped with a blank face at the knowledge that his day would likely be lasting another twelve hours or so. She felt exhausted herself, but the burning anger at her own failures and the loss of everything they had built fuelled an overdrive which she hoped would last until things got even slightly better than they were.

Maintaining their single-file progress across country, the rooftops became more clearly defined as they approached.

Clearing a small village shop which seemed to have been largely untouched, they began the tiring, repetitive cycle which would be their daily routine for the coming days. She helped herself to a few cans of overpriced energy drinks, the type crammed full of sugar and caffeine, and chugged most of a can down in one go. She tossed another to Paul, who did the same. Stuffing their bags with all they could find, they moved back outside with hopes of finding transport.

HOW QUICKLY LUCK CAN CHANGE

Leah even began to hum a tune to herself as she scanned the views from behind the bulletproof glass of their new ride. Their plan had been changed again, having found a mass of supplies to load onto their newly acquired and very capable vehicles. They had fuel for weeks of hard travel, and they elected to stick to the land bridge between continental Europe and Africa. That meant taking a leisurely drive through the Middle East, not a prospect many had fully considered.

The sense of joy and feeling refreshed by their resupply and the exciting new vehicle fleet was shattered within minutes as they crested a hill to look down on a blocked road.

Not just a blocked road like they had encountered so many times since the sudden collapse of everything, but an obvious and deliberate roadblock.

A huge truck had been driven quite intentionally into the middle of the road with another mirroring it from the opposite side. Between the two was another smaller truck. That flash of realisation that something wasn't right made Dan instantly lift off the accelerator pedal.

Recognising that the middle truck still had inflated tyres made him hit the brakes. Another second staring at the blatantly man-made obstruction made him snatch up the radio and call out to the other vehicles to turn around. They had rehearsed this in theory with all the drivers of their convoy: if the lead vehicle called a problem, then Mitch at the tail would spin around and become point while the heavier vehicles performed their own slow turns. Dan would then take position at the back until they regrouped.

As Dan spun the large armoured vehicle around, far more easily than its sheer size would dictate was possible due to the four-wheeled steering platform, he was met instantly with the brake lights of the vehicles in front. Not good. There must be another obstruction behind them. Hesitating between staying to protect the rear and wanting to lead from the front, he hovered his foot over the throttle for a few seconds before the radio crackled again into life.

"Attack rear! Attack rear!" barked Mitch's voice.

Decision made, Dan floored the right-hand pedal and surged past the heavier trucks. Quickly overtaking the stranded convoy, he pulled wide to get a better view and saw that they had rolled straight into a classic ambush: obstruction at the front, cut-off at the rear. What came next didn't need explaining; where they were sitting would now become a killing ground.

Unless the ambushers weren't prepared for a ruthless bastard with questionable mental health driving a bombproof truck.

The vehicle the attackers had used to cut off their escape had been poorly selected. A soft-skinned truck not unlike their old scavenging vehicles with an open side spanned most of the tarmac and was occupied with half a dozen men shooting at them.

No hesitation, Dan knew what he was going to do. Keeping his foot planted and reaching over forty miles an hour, he glanced to his right as he passed Mitch and Adam, both flat on the ground and pouring automatic fire at the barricade in short, controlled bursts.

Looking ahead again, he saw one of the men spasm and fall like a puppet whose strings had been cut. Stitched through the torso by the return fire, the man lost control of his legs but kept his finger on the trigger of his rifle as he fell. At least one other attacker was killed as he unknowingly emptied the remainder of his magazine into his comrades.

Those who had scrambled for safety were spared no mercy. No sooner had they escaped one violent death, another bore down on them through almost four tonnes of armoured vehicle.

One man stood fixed to the spot, unable to move through fear and the realisation of his imminent death. Dan was struck by how dishevelled he looked as he stood rooted to the concrete. His clothes were torn and dirty, his hair and beard long and wild. As he still considered the difference in their appearances, Dan hit him full in the chest with the front of his vehicle, crushing him instantly into the stationary truck.

It was an unfair fight. Their Foxhound versus a small truck. Bulletproof glass against thin fibreglass. Their well-executed plan was suddenly a chaotic shambles as the cruel solution obliterated the blocking vehicle. Bodywork, wheels and bodies flew in all directions as though they had exploded instead of being hit by another car.

Inside the Foxhound, and after Dan's shouted warning to hold tight, there was an air of anticlimax. They had barely been slowed down by the savage impact, and the wreckage around them didn't equate to the buffeting they had expected to feel.

Forty-five seconds from happy progress to the all-too-familiar sensation of surging adrenaline.

The road was open, the convoy fled, and the bubble of safety and excitement was utterly burst. Forty-five seconds to remind them that until they found a place to call home, until they were no longer nomads in an unknown place, they would never really be safe.

THE ENDLESS CYCLE OF HARD WORK

They stank. They were dirty, exhausted and none of them had managed to properly wash in days. Exposure during daylight at a water source was risky, not that they had come across much in the way of running water, and what precious little bottled water they found could not be wasted on ablutions.

As a result, the cramped vehicle they shared held an unpleasant and eye-watering aroma. Even with the windows down as they wound their ponderous way south, the fresh air did little to negate the stinging smell from their unwashed bodies. They didn't speak much other than to point out hazards or potential scavenging sites or to change drivers.

The small three-door hatchback Chris had nursed into reluctant life was showing a quarter tank of fuel, and the tortured noises from the engine bay made all of them wonder which would expire first. Still, it was better than walking. Slightly.

The overgrown hedgerows allowed occasional glimpses of a world they once knew being slowly eroded and reclaimed: a road sign here, half obscured by foliage; a streetlamp there, swamped and swathed in creeping ivy. One of these occasional glimpses told them they had progressed into another county, this time Dorset after Gloucestershire and Somerset and Wiltshire, on the halting trek towards open water and their continental destination.

No sooner had Lexi absorbed this landmark and begun to consult the road atlas taken from a fuel station's magazine racks did the car give a pained shudder. A murderous screeching noise emanated from the front, followed by an impossibly loud bang. Paul killed the engine, dropped it out of gear into neutral and let the expired car roll to a steaming stop. Silence reigned, as they were all too exhausted to speak.

"That'll be us walking again, then," said Chris in an almost nonchalant voice from the back.

With a resigned sigh, Lexi opened the door on its protesting hinges and began the process of tightening her equipment and strapping the bag to her back. The others followed suit, wordlessly preparing for yet another walk of unknown distance.

Tiredness made them complacent. It made Lexi simply too uncaring to enforce discipline and maintain their ordered march in wary single file. Soon, all four were trudging side by side down the road as though the prospect of meeting any threat were an inescapable inevitability.

As this cloud of unawareness descended on them, bizarrely their spirits lifted.

"What do you think happened to everyone?" asked Melissa to nobody in particular.

"I don't know," replied Chris, "but we've probably pissed enough people off to warrant a bit of bad karma."

"What the fuck is that supposed to mean?" interjected Paul, but the force of his words possessed no real gravity. "I mean, we've been the dominant ones since this all started, so there was bound to be someone bigger than us out there. Pissing about in a helicopter probably didn't help either," he finished patiently.

They absorbed this in silence, their minds opening up to the concept of their potential arrogance.

"How would the helicopter make us worse?" asked Melissa, genuinely confused by his emerging theory.

"It's like those sci-fi programmes," he explained. "You know, when aliens attack the earth because we've made some big leap in technology. Like we were saying that we were ready for the next level or something."

Lexi involuntarily scoffed at the mention of aliens and planetary invasions, which didn't gain her any favour with Chris.

"So you felt we were safe then?" he asked her rhetorically. "You think that just because we thought we were doing the right thing that others would just be like 'hey, they're good guys so let's just leave them alone and do our own thing'?"

She thought about that. "No," she said carefully, "that's not what I'm saying. In fact, I'm starting to agree with you."

The other three exchanged a look.

"How's that, then?" Paul asked her.

"I mean that we got comfortable," she said, a small injection of passion entering her words. "We probably were arrogant, and we probably all thought that because we'd survived everything so far that we were too big to take down. Look at the facts: everyone who has come at us has lost. Badly. We've wiped out three other groups and left literally no survivors... Did *they* think they deserved that?"

An awkward silence held them all for another hundred yards of walking.

"We didn't even have any defences in place on the farm," said Chris, "and Dan's 'nobody holds a gun except who I choose' was never questioned. Did you notice that everyone who left was carrying one? If we'd all had training and everyone was armed, then we could have had better security and whoever it was who took away our home might not have had such an easy time of it. No; he spent all his time with his dog and his woman and that scary-as-shit kid he turned into a killer."

At the growing criticism of Dan, Lexi tensed.

Her pride stung by the abuse of his rules and protocols, she turned on the farmer and looked him in the eye, ready to fly into a staunch defence of the man and everything he had done for them.

But the words deserted her, just as Dan had.

Her mouth opened and closed a few times as she fought with herself and her loyalties. Those loyalties were being rigorously tested now, and she found that when the shine of Dan's charismatic leadership had worn off, then maybe, just maybe, she agreed with what Chris was trying to say.

Without a word, she turned back and carried on walking.

She remained about ten steps ahead of the others as they continued the muttered conversation. Her fuming anger at herself, at Chris, at Dan and at whoever had taken away their home clouded her senses.

Those senses, even when tired, would have easily detected the sound of others talking long before it was too late.

From the hedgerow ahead of her emerged two men carrying shotguns, making her freeze and turn to look behind her.

Another two men there, similarly armed, were advancing on the others who were still lost in conversation. She spun back and raised her rifle as she shouted a warning for them to stay back.

"Whoa! Easy there!" said a voice from her right side. "No harm intended, boys; put your guns down now."

Lexi fought to control her breathing as she switched aim between the multiple targets.

The man who spoke walked towards her, remaining at an unthreatening distance as he spoke.

"We heard that engine coming miles away," he said kindly as he held his huge hands wide in a gesture of openness. "I've met people dressed like you two before, only they were in a better state than you are, I dare say."

So much competing information swam around in Lexi's brain that it was hard to concentrate and get everything in order. Before she could formulate any plan, the man spoke again.

"Come on, you look like you could do with a cup of tea."

Up close, she could see he was a big man, but his soft charm hid that fact unless you cared to look closely. He had kind eyes, a wide smile and huge hands. She thought he looked like someone she could trust. She wanted to trust him. She wanted to trust anyone right then, if only to feel safe again.

She lowered her rifle and stood straight, trying to regain her dignity despite being filthy with greasy hair and very aware of her own odour.

"Lexi," she introduced herself, then nodded to the other three and named them in turn.

The smiling man tentatively reached out a large hand to shake hers. She took it, her own small hand being instantly engulfed in a powerful grip which made her think that the rough, calloused brown skin around her own could do some real damage if he chose to do so.

The broad smile seemed very genuine, and Lexi felt a wave of emotion overcome her, almost as though they had been saved. Tears pricked her eyes at the relief and exhaustion.

"Tea?" the big man said once more, relieving the awkward tension with the most British of subject changes.

They followed him a short distance down the road until they met up with others around a Land Rover. As the vehicle came fully into sight, Lexi's eyes grew wide with shock. The extra tank on the roof rack and the bullet score mark above the windscreen all seemed so familiar.

That shock turned to fear, and that fear in turn transformed into rage.

Too close to the big man to step back and raise her rifle, she instead wrapped her left arm around his neck and whipped the Glock from the holster on her vest. Yanking his head back as far as she could given the David and Goliath size difference between them, she pressed the muzzle into the side of his head.

"Where did you get that car?" she screamed at him. "Where did you get it?"

Confusion reigned among everyone else. Paul raised his own gun, prompting Chris and Melissa to follow suit, but they were surrounded by the rest of the group with shotguns. Nobody really knew what to do, and an awkward stalemate hung heavy for a few seconds.

The big man was calm and could easily have stood up straight and overpowered the girl. Only he didn't, because the shock and her reaction was his fault. He blamed himself for not acting on his instincts that he knew where these people had come from. As soon as she recognised the Land Rover, he knew who she was. Where she had come from.

And he knew that their mutual friend had given him the vehicle, but she didn't, not yet.

Remaining very still, he answered her with a slow and clear response.

"Dan gave it to me," he said.

She froze, slowly absorbing the information into her fatigued and sleep-deprived brain. Gently, she relaxed the ineffective grip on his neck and moved the gun away. Holding it pointed towards the ground, she stepped back and allowed the man she had attacked to stand tall once more.

Rubbing his neck where she had hauled him down, he smiled again, waving his comrades away with a subtle gesture. Guns were lowered and everyone's personal space returned to an uninvaded state.

"Like I said earlier," he said with an open grin, "I've met people dressed like you before. That's where I got the truck, after I helped them."

A sob escaped Lexi's mouth, and it was quickly stifled. The shock and relief of knowing Dan and the others had been here, had met this man, overtook her emotions. She suddenly felt so very tired.

"You helped them?" she asked through tear-blurred eyes.

"We helped each other, more like," he answered. "They didn't need this anymore, so I inherited it. Allow me to start again. I'm Simon, and last time I saw your friends, they were way out to sea."

THE RAGE TO OVERCOME

Dan had driven hard away from the site of their attempted ambush, eyes moving as though they were plugged into the mains, looking for other threats and barking orders to the others in the car and over the radio.

After a few miles, to be sure they weren't being directly pursued, he called a stop away from the main road and posted Mitch and Adam to watch their rear after quickly checking on them. The only casualty was a ventilated windscreen on the Land Rover. The potential of losing a vehicle this early on was a blow, but going back for another was now out of the question.

Calling the others in, he explained what had happened. He didn't realise it then, but the hype he still felt from the adrenaline was pouring out of him as pure anger. Everyone present was made to feel that they were in some way responsible for what had happened, as though they were all collectively to blame, when in fact he blamed none of them. He blamed the hideous state of humanity. He blamed those people for attacking them when there was no sensible reason to do it. He was angry that people shot first and looted later, instead of having a simple conversation or offering trade.

He was appalled at the extreme lack of good manners.

His words were harsh and full of rage; his voice was raised but at the same time his hands shook from fear and adrenaline and his heart beat so hard that he could hear his own pulse in his ears. As his anger at the behaviour of other humans abated, he saw his most faithful follower sliding away from the group wearing a look like he'd left a steaming present on his master's new carpet.

Seeing his dog afraid made him stop. He was making others feel afraid too. They should be afraid, he thought, just not afraid of him. Dan was doing this all wrong.

Clicking his fingers and calling Ash to him, he bent down to fuss the huge animal and reassure him that it was OK now.

Standing up again, he began the harder task of reassuring his human followers that it was going to be OK for them too.

"We have a hard day driving ahead of us now," he said to the group, more softly now, "but we need to put as much space between us and here as we can. Everyone take a break while we look at the maps, but just stay close to the vehicles!"

Catching Leah's eye, he walked towards where she had laid the map out on the bonnet of a long-deceased car.

"Head back west, go down through Italy," she said simply. Marie, Neil, Jimmy and Jack joined them, and Leah repeated her stance on their navigation.

"Best way," replied Neil. "If we're meeting people like that in Germany and the last lot in Belgium, then I doubt we'll find a better reception when we hit the Gaza strip, do you?"

Agreement rippled through the small assembly. For want of a better plan which didn't involve fighting their way across a thousand miles, they decided to head back in the general direction they had come from.

Dan's anger was still running high, so he took himself away for a solitary cigarette. Now convinced of his own innocence in the recent bad mood, Ash dutifully followed to lope at his flank, nose to the ground and ears up. Breathing heavily to purge the last of the fear-induced chemicals from his body, Dan concentrated on lowering his heart rate and returning to a sense of balance.

Healthy balance was not something Dan experienced often nowadays. In fact, a healthy state of mind was now something as fleeting as a burst of fear or anger had been in the past. He was tired, so unbelievably emotionally and physically exhausted that he could just curl up where he was and cry.

Only he couldn't do that anymore. As much as he wanted to lie down in the foetal position and wait for all the bad things to pass him by, he simply couldn't afford the delay. People's lives depended on him, including the ones who meant the most to him. His frustration at the world threatened his eyes with tears, not of sadness, but of anguish at the futility of the world. A footfall behind him made him spin around and place an instinctive hand on his carbine.

Leah had got close before he heard her, not intentionally, as she knew better than to creep up on an armed man who lived on the edge, but because of her ingrained sense of stealth.

"Steady," she said in a slightly mocking impression of him. The levity was enough to bring him down from the last step of emotional reaction and articulate how he felt.

"What the hell was all that about?" he asked her.

She opened her mouth to speak, then considered the discussion she had recently with Emma about people being rhetorical. She closed her mouth again, guessing rightly that Dan hadn't finished.

"I mean, what did they want with us? Supplies? Weapons? Why couldn't they just walk up and ask us?" he ranted on, cursing the world in general and lamenting that conflict was as natural to the human race as breathing. "We're just destined to destroy each other, I reckon," he said glumly.

Leah guessed he had finished now. She knew that he liked to get on his soapbox and say things like this from time to time, and she had learned to let it run. Her mind drifted off a little as she pondered if he spent his downtime making up these speeches.

Stepping closer, she placed a hand on his shoulder. There was no awkwardness between them, which was strange, as neither were emotionally open people, and Dan raised his eyes to meet hers.

"Believe me when I say this, because I love you, but you seriously need to man up." A sarcastic smirk tickled the corner of her mouth; she clearly wanted to laugh at her own humour.

Dan looked at her, burning an intense gaze through her until she could no longer take it and burst out laughing. He laughed with her and stood to hug her.

"Point taken, you little shit," he said warmly, then turned and walked back towards the vehicles. "And I love you too. Just don't go thinking I'm increasing your pocket money or letting you stay up late," he said over his shoulder as he paced away.

Leah's smile remained as she watched him go. She knew she had, or at least used to have, a father. Her mum used to talk about him every so often, just not very nicely. She had never actually known her own dad, not properly anyway, and if she really concentrated, she could only just recall what he looked like.

Nothing like Dan. She wondered again what he had been like before, and if her mum had met him whether he could've become her dad for real.

"Pointless thought," she said to herself wistfully, "it is what it is." And she was happy with that. She had a dad now and a hairy brother who drooled in the car and was known for his tendency to bite. She had a mum of sorts. Soon she would have a younger brother or sister too.

Then the realisation of that hit her. She steeled herself and walked back to the group, back to the mission, and back to her dysfunctional family.

"Woman up," she muttered to herself as she put her game face back on.

After all, she had a reputation to uphold.

PLAN B

"Well, it's probably more of a plan Y by now," retorted Mitch as Dan circled their Land Rover and assessed the damage.

"You know what I mean," Dan said distractedly.

He saw the four crazed bullet holes dotted across the windscreen in a curving arc, marvelling at their luck that nobody was hurt. Not strictly true, as both Adam and Mitch had suffered cuts to their hands and faces from the glass. The four bullets which had entered the cab had harmlessly impacted the bags and boxes stacked behind the front seats, and he saw how one had gouged a piece off the passenger's side head restraint and exposed the uncomfortably cheap, off-beige foam stuffing.

As he checked the rest of the vehicle and saw numerous scrapes where rounds had ricocheted off the metal and slashed away the green paint, Mitch began to conduct repairs.

Ripping off pieces of duct tape, Mitch began to seal the holes in the glass before moving on to wrap the seat and shut in the escaping foam. He saw Dan's amused look and explained.

"Land Rovers: they go anywhere and you can fix most things with duct tape," he said with a smile. "Well, for a while anyway."

Dan chuckled. "OK, so what's plan Y or whatever we've got to if it dies on us?" he asked.

"Switch the supplies into the big wagon and we go on top of the other vehicles as lookouts?" Mitch replied.

"Sounds cold," Dan answered, "and uncomfortable."

Mitch merely shrugged away the concepts as insignificant.

Stepping closer, Dan asked him a question in a hushed tone. "How did your boy do?" he muttered.

"Good enough," came the quiet answer. "He had to change his trousers, but that's not uncommon, as you know. Didn't you piss your pants in your first contact?" Mitch asked Dan innocently.

"As a matter of fact, I did. Some forgotten village in the Balkans in the pitch-black. Didn't know what the hell was going on!" he answered quietly with a private smile. "What about you?"

"You're kidding, right?" Mitch said with a wide grin. "No chance, mate!"

Annoyed and amused by being duped, Dan gave him a single-worded insult in good humour and walked away to find Adam and reassure him.

As he walked, he tried to remember the first post-contact pep talk he had received, delivered by a sergeant major with an impressive growth of big pork chop sideburns. He'd never forget those chops: as hilarious as they were to look at, the man wearing them was not someone you would laugh at. Or in front of, or anywhere there was a chance he could hear you. *They shoot at us and we shoot at them, lad,* barked the fierce, loud voice from the depths of his memory. *In the end we win, because we're better. If you end up dead, then you'll know you weren't good enough.*

From those memories, he saw the twenty-year-old Dan, fresh-faced and unburdened by years of pain and distrust, trying his hardest to hold his chin from quivering. You didn't show weakness in front of the brutally hard man, even with comedy facial hair disguising his look of pure malevolence while addressing one so young and inexperienced.

Still, that was how it had been for generations, and probably would have been for years to come if the whole world hadn't been turned upside down; children were bullied into conflict under a flag by older bullies who had been bullied themselves.

That was over-simplified, he allowed, and overly harsh. He had felt a burning pride at serving his country, at going to war and being part of one of the best, if not by any means the biggest, gangs on the planet. If only he could speak to that twenty-year-old now, he could dispense some valuable advice.

As he wandered, he tried to remember what Adam had been before; was he a plumber? No, something to do with bathroom fittings or tiles. It didn't really matter. What they were before held little or no relevance to what they were now.

Finding Adam carrying his heavy bag back towards the newly ventilated Land Rover and wearing an embarrassed look, Dan tried to soften his face to convey a sense of unjudging empathy. Adam dropped his bag and stood awkwardly in his clean trousers, broadcasting an obvious juxtaposition between the clean black cotton and the travel-stained top and equipment vest.

Dan waved Ash away from him to sniff at a nearby hedgerow while he lit a cigarette to give himself thinking time.

"First one's a big milestone," he said as he exhaled, trying to sound nonchalant about it. He was just about to launch into a superior-sounding speech about dealing with the aftermath of a contact and deliver some words of wisdom when the truth of the situation hit him like a brick in the chest. All he was missing were the big chops and the obvious loathing of other human beings, but other than that, he was the sergeant major preaching to the new recruit.

Suddenly lost for words, he slapped a hand on Adam's shoulder and walked away as he whistled for his dog.

He was just an old soldier pushing the next generation, only there was no flag now.

WARM SAFE PLACE

The cycle of the last nearly two weeks had been broken in relative style. They had bathed in warm water, rinsing away the filth and stink of the hard travelling. They were dressed in clean clothes, took the time to clean their equipment and all the while were given hot drinks.

Real hot drinks. Tea with actual milk, not the powdery stuff they had come to barely tolerate, which left a film on their teeth and had a nasty habit of accumulating into chewy lumps. Real milk. From cows.

It was a small comfort, but one they rarely had even before they lost their home.

With the drinks came food, and after the scraps they had survived on for the previous fortnight, that too was like the richest ambrosia.

Now fed, clean and rehydrated, they sat with their hosts and Lexi tried to apologise again for earlier.

"I just panicked a bit," she explained to Simon for the fourth or fifth time since they met. "I saw the truck and assumed or something…" she said as her voice trailed away.

Simon held up a big hand to ward off any further clumsy attempts at an apology which he felt wasn't necessary. His broad smile beamed at her again, making her embarrassment even worse than before. "It's fine, my dear. Honestly," he said with a small laugh at her discomfort. "It was actually us who pointed guns at your friends when we first met them."

His smile faded away at the thought that of the group who first met Dan and Mitch, only he remained alive. His smile wavered further when he saw Lexi's face drop at the mention of the others.

"I think it's time you told me what happened, don't you?" he asked kindly. Lexi's face remained pointed at the ground, so Chris interjected.

"The one you met, Dan, he was our leader in a way," he said to Simon, "but a couple of months back, he decided to leave for bloody Africa to try and save Marie – she's his woman and was another sort of leader – because she's pregnant and their weird scientist girl thinks she knows a way to make the babies survive." His own voice wavered as the painful memories of his own stillborn child surged to the surface like a breaching whale. He swallowed and went on. "I lost a baby," he said, pausing to cough and straighten himself, "and my woman too. She went away with them."

Simon nodded with him as he spoke, keeping a respectful silence. All of this he knew from speaking to Dan anyway, but in a small way he was enjoying hearing their story from the perspective of the nonbelievers. It would have been far more entertaining had the story not been so tragic.

Simon had heard the arrival of the helicopter in the harbour and later spoke with Dan about Steve and marvelled at their luck in finding a pilot and a working aircraft. To hear Dan relay Steve's fears that it wouldn't last long become reality in Chris's blunt description of the terrible crash made the whole tale become sadder by the minute.

Lexi picked up the story again after Chris became too emotional to continue, and she spoke about how they had started to lose cohesion, to come undone at the seams without the ones who had left. She told him of her own failings. Of how she couldn't step up in the circumstances to fill both Dan's and Steve's shoes and how she retreated into a permanent state of hostility towards everyone. She told him of the suddenness of the attack, of her burning anger at the betrayal of the twins, and of their quickly made choice to flee instead of fighting. It stung her how easily she had made that decision, and only pure chance had led to Chris and Melissa being with them.

She blamed herself for the uncontested arrival of the twins, saying that she should have tried harder to retain control, that if she had then none of it would have happened and they would still have a home.

"That's utter bollocks," growled Chris from behind her, making her turn around to look at his angry, tear-filled eyes. "That's bollocks and you know it. Stop trying to blame yourself," he said. "You think even Dan and all the others could've stopped whoever it was wiping us out? No. Look at how many of them there were; we were outnumbered and all of them were armed. We'd have been slaughtered if Dan was there and tried to fight them off. So stop feeling sorry for yourself." With that, he rose and walked away for some privacy.

Lexi was shocked by the outburst, but she was beginning to agree with Chris's feelings. They hadn't stood a chance. They would have had to build defences and man them 24/7 to have stopped a force that size. As much as she agreed with that, her ingrained defence of Dan and his policies still ran deep, and she felt obligated to object to laying the full blame on their saviour who had abandoned them.

Her mouth opened but she found herself unable to articulate those feelings with any coherent sequence of words. She closed her mouth and looked at Simon, hoping he would understand her confusion to further explain her actions.

The big man stirred himself in his seat. "Would it help if I told you what he did for me?" he said, setting out the scene without waiting for a reply.

Almost without emotion, he told them of meeting Dan and the subsequent attack on his camp. Speaking in a quiet monotone, he told them of how he and his friend had been rescued. Of how their friends worked desperately to save a man's life. Of how he felt when they couldn't, and he realised that all the men who had trusted him, had followed him, were all dead now. He told them of how Dan had helped him gather fuel, given him the Land Rover, and then set sail across the Channel with hope.

Aboard *Hope*, to be precise.

He didn't tell them that he had turned back after an hour of driving. That he had hidden the Land Rover and crept to the seafront under cover of darkness where he lay in wait until his patience paid off and he was able to exact a brutal and murderous revenge on the man who had hurt him so badly.

He would take that story with him to the grave, because to tell another soul about it would make it real, and if it were real then he was a savage man who was just as capable of murder as he was of tending livestock or growing crops.

He didn't want to think of himself like that, so those two days and two nights were consigned to a locked vault in his memory.

He looked up, slowly waking from his reverie to see the assembled faces watching him. Waiting for more.

But there was no more that he would share, so his mask of a broad smile returned and he did what he did best: he changed the subject.

"So, how can we help you?" he asked them.

The four outsiders looked at each other, unsure of what they really wanted. If Lexi were pushed to guess, she'd think that Chris and Melissa would stay with Simon and his group. Become farmers again and live in peace. She hoped Paul would stay with her, whatever she decided.

"Can you help us get to France?" asked Chris, breaking the silence and shocking Lexi. Simon took a sip of his tea and smiled at them. "I can do one better," he said, pausing to drain his cup and flick the dregs away on the grass. "I'll come with you."

THE VOID

The official title was Camp Bravo, which he thought was predictably unimaginative. On deeper reflection from the uncomfortable hospital bed, the name given to their new home – irrespective of their personal wishes – was wholly indicative of the personality of the man in charge.

His complete lack of one, more like.

He struck his first camp, moved to a new site and attached the moniker "Bravo" to imply it was the second place. The next letter in the alphabet. A to B.

It was precisely that stiff lack of personality which made almost everyone at the camp despise their leader. The man who strutted around, constantly flanked by no less than four armed men at all times.

Dan would never have needed a bodyguard detail, Steve thought with amusement. Even if there were people who wanted to do him harm, he would still refuse protection and meet whatever threat he faced head on. Sometimes that attitude was a failing too, but in light of their current contrast, Dan could do no wrong.

If he were there. Or even knew where they were.

Steve had to resign himself to the fact that they were part of the bigger machine now. Someone else's machine. They had been swallowed up just as much as a dozen other groups had been, and now they were part of Camp Bravo.

For Steve, life felt like a void, like he had fallen into an empty pit with no bottom, no sides and no way out. The pain he experienced didn't help, nor did the regular doses of opiates he was given. He spent days, or it could have been weeks, in a daze interrupted only by crippling waves of pain and occasional overheard snippets of talk. At times, he didn't know if he was awake, or even alive, and his fogged brain made little sense of what he heard and saw.

He realised he was becoming more aware of his surroundings, although he had no idea how long he had been there. He had grown a beard, giving him the estimate of at least four weeks since the crash.

The crash.

It came back to him again like an electric shock.

The noise.

The terror.

The pain.

Closing his eyes tightly to try and squeeze away the images and feelings in his head, he breathed steadily to calm himself.

Factory reset. *Open your eyes*, he told himself mentally, *deal with what's happening now. Open your eyes.*

Looking up at the stained ceiling, he tried to place his surroundings. Draughty, with a plastic feel to the room. Stale. A portacabin? The smell was terrible, a cross between rotting meat and chemicals.

He realised in horror that most of the smell was him. His clothes were stiff where he had soiled himself and it had dried into the fabric. A film of dried sweat covered his skin and left an unpleasantly sticky feel. Silently, he began a top-to-toe survey of his body.

Thinking firstly of his head, he felt the throbbing pain emanating down his neck and the tingling area of numbness behind his right ear. Moving down his aching neck, he tensed arms and fingers until a deep breath sent a sudden stab of agony through his ribcage.

Best not to try that again, he thought.

Hips, waist, legs all tensed in turn until the sensation of his lower right leg fully returned. The lancing, searing jolt of agony fired a full salvo up his leg and continued along up his spine where his brain registered the sensation and threatened to return him to unconsciousness.

As his rapid breathing began to calm and the tears stopped flowing down his cheeks, he summoned the courage to try and move again. *It's only pain*, he thought to himself, but this kind of pain couldn't be used in conjunction with the word *only*.

Forcing his weakened body to exert the energy, he pushed down on the thin mattress to raise his upper body, gasping with the effort as he turned the movement into sitting up. Burst sores on his back left his raw skin exposed as the scabs stayed put on the dirty sheets and his atrophied muscles quivered with the exertion until he was upright.

Pausing to catch his breath, he looked down at the thin blanket covering his legs. Like ripping off a dressing, he threw it aside quickly to expose his lower limbs. He didn't know what he expected, but seeing a blackened and swollen shin through the straps of an immobilisation boot, he knew instantly that he had broken it badly and that someone had fixed it with a degree of skill he didn't possess.

Details flooded back to him: Lizzie and Alice, more pain and the bliss that overcame him when the injections were given, and the noise and panic when their home was taken from them.

He sensed that he had been left with the minimum of care to see if he recovered, although the empty drips of ampicillin on the stand next to his bed told him that they didn't want him dead, just in pain.

Sitting on the edge of the bed, he caught sight of his reflection in a scratched mirror on the wall. He looked like a prisoner of war being repatriated: emaciated and dirty.

"You're awake," said a voice from the other side of the room, making Steve jump in fright. A stocky man in pale-green scrubs was sitting on a plastic chair in the corner of the room. He gently closed the book he was reading and placed it down with an air of reverence on the table next to him before looking up and regarding Steve. He smiled at him, although not convincingly.

"Don't ask me any questions because I probably don't know the answer and I wouldn't be allowed to tell you even if I did," he said in a distinct accent as he stood and stretched, revealing thick arms and a broad chest as he uncoiled like a resting animal.

Steve regarded him as best as he could manage, trying to piece together the words he wanted to say and croak them out of his dry throat. Of everything he could have asked the man, he was most curious about his uncommon accent.

"You're," he began, before coughing in sudden pain. He regained his breath as the man strode effortlessly across the creaking floor and picked up a bottle of water. He tossed it to Steve, who fumbled the catch and winced as the bottle struck his ribs.

No soft touch here, he thought. Drinking greedily, he wiped his mouth and tried again. "You're South African?" he asked the man.

"Oh? How did you guess?" he replied with a grin of sarcasm.

Unsure if he was being toyed with, Steve chose his next words with greater care. "I mean, your accent, it's not very common–"

The man cut him off with a wave of his hand. "I'm fucking with you, man. Relax!"

Hoping that the joviality was genuine, Steve did what he was told not to do. "How long have I been here?" he asked, receiving a reproving glare in response.

The man said nothing, just walked up to Steve and placed one hand on his forehead to shine a light in both eyes in turn.

He muttered softly as he worked. "There's a guard right outside the door," he said as he made a pretence of checking Steve's pulse and looking at his watch when in fact his fingers were nowhere near the artery in his neck. "Whoever you were, you've really upset someone."

"I stole a helicopter from Richards," Steve whispered in response.

The man stopped and looked him directly in the eye, a slow smile creeping the corners of his mouth upwards. "Well, my friend," he said quietly, "you just became my newest hero!" Stepping back and raising his voice to normal levels, he addressed Steve for the benefit of listening ears. "Right, you stink, so I need to get you to the showers. My name is Jan. I'm the orderly in the hospital wing." He pronounced the J as a Y.

"Jan?" Steve asked.

"Trust me, man, you wouldn't be able to pronounce my full name!"

With that, he was helped to his feet and given crutches. They were slightly too short for him, and his wasted muscles made moving very hard work. With a great degree of difficulty and a lot of help from Jan, he made it to the shower, where he sat on a plastic chair and washed away the blood and filth.

Clean and clothed, he was returned to the portacabin, where fresh bed sheets had replaced the old ones. The smell mostly remained.

Out of breath from the effort of moving, Steve lay back on the bed with the back raised as his chest heaved to repay the oxygen taken from his muscles.

"I'll get you some food," said Jan, having returned to a more genial mood now out of sight of the guards. "Stay here," he said as he left the room.

Steve's head spun from the effort of moving only a matter of metres.

"Don't worry, pal," he said to the ceiling, "I'm not going anywhere."

DOG-TIRED

Two days of driving slowly, scouting ahead and making camp for the night in a carefully selected position made for very slow progress.

They were all tired, tempers were fraying and mistakes were being made. Dan drove for three hours in a trance-like state, leading the convoy onwards until Jack asked irritably over the radio why they were travelling north.

In her exhaustion, Leah had called the wrong turn and nobody else had noticed. Dan fought down his overreaction, swallowed the tirade he was about to throw at her and reminded himself that the teenage girl beside him was just as tired as he was. *Forget the protocol*, he thought to himself, and he signalled a stop.

Unbidden, Leah climbed out of the big truck and stretched her muscles before hefting her rifle and climbing up to the roof to keep watch.

Dan walked along the exhausted convoy as his group climbed stiffly down from vehicles and tried to ease out their discomfort. Tired smiles greeted him as Ash trotted dutifully alongside, stopping at every third wheel to ensure it was adequately watered. As he reached the back of the convoy, he saw that Mitch and Adam had pulled their vehicle up a little way back and slewed it slightly across the tarmac as an obstacle to any pursuit. His purpose in seeking them out was to ask for a rearguard, but on reaching them, he saw both sitting on the roof of their vehicle facing south. Behind them, a small camp kettle was already brewing water.

A smile crept on Dan's face, despite his bone-weary somnolence: always trust in a soldier's ability to find a hot drink. Deciding to leave them in peace, he turned and headed back to the others, satisfied that his best fighters were in place to protect them.

Everywhere he looked, he saw people at the point of exhaustion through travel, and these weren't even the ones doing sentry duty or driving their sturdy convoy all over the continent. Just as the annoyance crept in, it was supplemented with a hint of repulsion as he saw Henry trotting towards him. Trying his hardest not to seem overtly annoyed at the boy's presence, he waited for whatever doting token of adoration was about to be heaped on him.

On seeing the boy's round face showing no signs of trying to impress him as he ran the short distance, the annoyance was turned into an immediate concern. Something was wrong.

"What is it?" Dan demanded of him angrily before the boy could even speak. The twenty-metre run had temporarily taken away his breath, and Dan's fear combined with tiredness threatened to bring on a rage that the boy did not deserve. Ignoring Henry's attempts at jabbering through the information, he strode purposefully past him and towards the front of the convoy where the commotion had started.

When his own vehicle came into sight, his heart dropped, releasing that all-too-familiar sense of dread, the cold feeling of a sudden drop and the instant burn in his muscles as the adrenaline took immediate effect.

He saw Kate kneeling awkwardly in the back of the armoured vehicle as others clamoured to see what was happening. Dan's worst fears were realised when he approached and heard the erstwhile paramedic's voice.

"Marie!" she said loudly. "Open your eyes. Look at me!"

Not bothering to shout a warning, he barrelled his way through the small crowd gathering, prompting shouts of alarm and pain as at least one person was knocked to the floor.

"What's wrong?" he growled at Kate as he reached the open door. She knew his aggression was the result of fear, his way of showing he had feelings other than being tired or hungry, but his inability to articulate grated on her. Like everyone, she was tired too and not in the mood to be barked at.

"I don't bloody know yet," she snapped at him savagely. "If you backed off, I might find out!"

Her incivility stopped him dead; he had barely heard her raise her voice in all the months he had known her. In other circumstances, he would have something to say; however, his fear left him dumb-struck. He reached in to put a hand on Marie's head, feeling her travel-greasy hair was hot to the touch.

Kate slapped his hand away, no longer bothering to acknowledge the presence of anyone there but her patient, then shone a small light in her eyes before feeling for her pulse in the rudimentary way.

Ten seconds of silence reigned, like a coincidental holding of breath for everyone present, until she pulled back her hand and moved to undo the harness buckle that kept Marie slumped into the uncomfortable seat.

"Help me get her out," Kate ordered. "She's fainted and probably dehydrated too."

The awkward and ungainly dance of moving an unconscious person seemed to take an eternity, but by the time Marie had been lifted clear of the truck, Dan turned to see that Neil – ever-reliable Neil – had organised an improvised stretcher with a sleeping bag on. She was gently laid on it, and to the quick-fire orders of Kate, she was lifted and carried away to the shade in the back of their largest truck.

Dan went to follow until Sera rounded on him in fury.

"No!" she snarled at him, jabbing a finger at his chest but serving only to jar her knuckle on the heavy ballistic vest he wore. Shaking away the pain she had just caused herself, she continued with her diatribe towards him, stepping forward as she spoke. "You want to help?" she said angrily, her voice rising as she spoke each word and staring at him through red-ringed eyes. "Then find us somewhere safe. Now. We can't all live on the road like this, especially not Marie because, if you didn't bloody realise, she is pregnant with your child." Another push to his chest made him step back further in horror at the sudden onslaught. "And if that doesn't make its way through your thick skull, then I might as well talk to HIM!"

With her last shouted word, she pointed to a confused and equally shocked Ash, who, sensing that he was now due for the same treatment, was abandoned by what remained of his courage. Grumbling a noise somewhere between a half-hearted growl and a whimper, he stumbled awkwardly backwards to seek the safety behind Dan's legs as though he could protect him from the relentless offensive.

Man and dog exchanged a look, then turned back to see their attacker storming angrily away. In her place came a quiet and placatory Neil who gently led him away.

Ash, sensing that they had survived an attack where their unrelenting duality had left so many foes vanquished, meekly followed as he threw one cautious glance backwards at Sera.

Neil stopped and rubbed his face, rough hands scratching on the long stubble on his cheeks. Like everyone, he was red-eyed and travel-weary to the point of exhaustion. Dan wasn't in the mood for a lecture, or an impression, or any of Neil's idiosyncrasies right then, so he turned to follow Marie.

"Before you go, mate," said Neil quietly. The low tone, the obvious lack of any humour and the sound of desperation made Dan turn back. "They're right," Neil said, stifling a yawn so big he had to wait seconds to finish his sentence. "We need to rest up somewhere. We can't keep travelling like this or we'll break."

"I bloody know," Dan said, snarling at him and speaking more harshly than he ever intended to and making Neil's point clear in just three words. Dan softened, relaxed his shoulders and took a breath. His equipment cut into him; everywhere his clothes touched him itched. His fingernails were dirty and cracked and he hadn't shaved in as long as he could remember. "I know," he said again, more calmly. "I'll figure it out, but now I'm going to make sure she's OK."

He turned and walked away. Neil thought for a second that he saw his friend stagger slightly as he went and he didn't even bother to call Ash to heel. The older man sighed in relief; having been volunteered by everyone to be the one who raised that very subject at the next opportunity, he had been saved the trouble by Marie. Neil turned his back to make the necessary preparations and make sure the million and four things he had to do were done. He cast an incredulous eye towards the patch of shade on the soft grass next to him.

Flat on his back, all four feet in the air and his tongue lolling out of one side of his mouth, Ash slept the deep, satisfied slumber of a dog with no concerns.

"Lucky bastard," Neil muttered as he left, not wanting to wake him up.

NOT-SO-FOND FAREWELLS

"So why would it work for us and not for them?" Paul asked for the third time in as many minutes. He wasn't getting it.

"Because," Chris explained patiently in a tone of voice bordering dangerously on the condescending, "we are going in one small vehicle and they had lots of people and big vehicles. That's why they took a boat."

The discussions of how they planned to get to the continent were taking too long to make. At every juncture, someone else had an opinion on how something should be done or what they would need to achieve it.

Lexi felt like she should take charge of it, like she had seen Dan do so many times: find a problem, ask what people thought, come up with a plan quickly and make it work. Only she knew with every cell in her body that she wasn't Dan, nor right now did she want to be thinking about him.

Simon and Chris were very much on the same level, but then again, they came from very similar backgrounds. Melissa was annoyingly quiet throughout and offered little in the way of opinion or assistance, and Paul, she sensed, was being deliberately obtuse to annoy Chris, who he felt had become a little too headstrong.

"Oh!" He feigned surprise at finally understanding the logic in the proposed plan. "So they couldn't get through the tunnel but we can?"

"Yes!" snapped Chris, taking the baited hook.

Simon seemed to know how the ensuing conversation would end, so he sat back with a small smile to watch.

"In that case," Paul said, dropping the ignorant act, "perhaps you can explain about the pressures on *'le chunnel'* after nearly a year and a half of neglect?"

Silence.

"Perhaps you know that the tunnels will be clear and we won't find ourselves reversing nearly thirty miles when we reach a dead end in the pitch-black and have seventy-odd metres of sea above our heads and no maintenance schedule to make sure we're not going to be crushed, or drowned, or any other of the hundred bloody ways we could die doing this?" Paul's voice had risen as he spoke, and had reached a shout by the time his diatribe had finished.

Now, in the embarrassed silence that followed, Paul sat back down and offered a more relaxed opinion on their proposed path.

"The Eurotunnel is an engineering masterpiece. It's one of only a few like it in the world, and if we don't find it already collapsing, in my opinion, then I don't want to be that far underground when it does."

He looked at everyone in turn, trying to bore his fears into them. Chris glared back, Melissa wasn't even looking at him, Simon simply smiled, and Lexi met his gaze and held it.

"Have we not taken risks before?" she asked quietly.

Paul simply stared at her, unable to comprehend that she wasn't supporting his argument.

"Pros and cons," she said, looking around at the others. "Weigh up the risks against the benefits. If it's still intact and if it's clear, then we could be in France in the exact vehicle we need with all our supplies in what, an hour? Less?"

Paul, being the best person qualified to answer the question, cleared his throat. "Under ninety minutes," he admitted grudgingly, "but there's a bucket-load of 'ifs' there."

"And *if*," she went on, "we find it blocked or full of water, then we find another way. But *if* we have a chance to get through in one piece and not have to scavenge vehicles and food and supplies on the other side, then we need to take it."

Simon still sat wearing an amused smile as he watched the play unfold. He knew there was a chance of a collapse, but he also knew how hard it would be to find a vehicle anywhere near as capable and well-quipped as the Land Rover Dan had given him. It was perfect for the journey they faced, other than it couldn't float, and finding a replacement would be next to impossible.

"Sounds like a plan to me!" Simon said happily.

Exasperated, Paul sat back heavily and made no show of hiding his annoyance at their engineering ignorance. Chris stayed quiet after having been embarrassed by Paul's rant and the subsequent argument.

"Then let's do it," Lexi said as she rose.

"I don't want to go," came a small voice. It came as no major surprise to Lexi, but the others stared at Melissa in shock. Chris was the first to speak.

"Why?" he asked, fumbling for more words. It was clear to both Paul and Lexi that he liked Melissa being around him, and ever since

Ana had turned away from Chris after the stillbirth, he had spent longer hours at the farm and subsequently more time with Melissa.

"Look at me!" she said tiredly and with a self-depreciating smile. "I'm no adventurer. I don't like carrying a gun with me everywhere. I just want to be safe and sleep at night."

She turned her smile towards Chris, telling those watching that she knew the real reason he wanted her to come.

"You could stay too, you know?" she said softly.

"No!" he said angrily, then let out a breath and seemed to shrink a little. "No," he said again more gently. "I want to look Dan in the face and tell him everything. I want to describe the crash to him. I want him to know what it felt like to lose our home. If I can do that and come back, then I will."

He picked up his rifle awkwardly and walked away.

Lexi and Paul followed at a respectable distance to talk to him, leaving Simon and Melissa alone.

"Why do you want to go?" she asked him in a subdued but curious tone.

Simon took a long breath to give him time to consider his answer. In truth, he found it too difficult to look people in the eyes when he alone of their loved ones returned from the expedition. His account of what had happened on the coast had holes, too many holes in fact, and he suspected that the rest of the group knew he was hiding something. That he was concealing a cold-blooded murder of one of their own, as traitorous and evil as he was, and that heavy burden was portrayed as secrecy.

He had lost their trust and had gained their suspicion, and that made for a lonely life.

He fixed the girl with a lopsided smile. "Nobody will miss me here," he said sadly, "and I have a slate to wipe clean."

AT ONE WITH NATURE

After the brief scare of Marie fainting and the desperately frayed nerves of everyone in their debilitated convoy, Dan reluctantly ceded to the demands of others to find a place to rest. Sera's hostility was softened by Kate's genuine plea that they could not continue as they were, and that was her medical opinion.

In truth, Dan took very little convincing that it was the right thing to do, but the questions of where and how long for were his major concerns.

To pick an unsafe or undependable position was to endanger the lives of everyone. To delay too long could jeopardise the lives of Marie and their baby.

Where they were would have to suffice for the night; another argument with Sera about moving Marie was an unwelcome prospect. Calling in Adam and Mitch to join Leah, Neil and himself, he laid out the proposal in the safety provided by Jack and Jimmy keeping watch at either end of the stationary convoy.

"We need a temporary site," he announced in hushed tones away from inquisitive ears. "Somewhere for a week's rest that can be defended." He let that sink in as he arched his back and was rewarded with a sickening crack of compressed vertebrae. Ignoring the disgusted look on Leah's face, he continued.

"At first light, I want you two," he said, pointing at Mitch and Neil, "to take the bikes and find the nearest place." The two men he chose were perfect for the task, as one would consider the group's needs and comfort while the other would assess it from an attacker's point of view.

Neither had any objections, and nobody had any questions. They were all simply too fatigued to care too much.

As the meeting ended and people went their separate ways, Leah followed Dan as he stiffly walked away the cramps in his muscles. Both sipped on hot coffee as they walked until Leah broke the silence.

"You should take it easy at your age," she said innocently, intentionally poking the bear for her own amusement.

"And you should be in school at your age," he retorted, "so looks like neither will be happening."

Fair enough, thought Leah, happy that she managed to force some humour out of him despite how lame it was.

Stopping to light a cigarette, he turned to the girl and assessed her. She was dirty, her hair was shiny with grease and he couldn't be sure which one of them was emanating the unpleasant stale body odour. It was probably him, he reckoned.

Deciding that he should make some kind of "I'm proud of you speech", he tried to find the words, but nothing came. He settled on telling her to get some rest before she took over sentry duty before first light. With a nod, she turned to leave and he called her back.

"You've got something on your vest," he said, pointing his index finger at her chest. Instinctively, she looked down only to be rewarded with the obvious and annoying finger poking her in the nose. Dan accompanied the gesture with a comedy "boop!" and earned himself a look somewhere between *Dad, you're so embarrassing* and *do that again and I will cut you.*

Pleased that he had elicited some humour in her response, Dan smiled at her and watched her walk away. Smoking in satisfied silence, he checked his watch to calculate if he could grab a couple of hours' sleep himself before he took over watch in the night.

At first light, both Dan and Leah, him at the rear and her at the head of the convoy, readied themselves for action.

Sunset and sunrise, and the hour either side of both.

The times for peak alertness, ingrained in Dan from a young age and passed on through tradition to Leah, for any sentry duty at night. When the sun was fully clear, Dan relaxed slightly to see that Mitch had joined him in a defensive position some distance away from the vehicle.

The instinct was more thoroughly ingrained in Mitch than any of the others.

Nodding to him, Dan sat up to make himself slightly more comfortable as Mitch and Neil began to unload the loud and ungainly motorbikes from their straps on the side of the fuel tanker. They hadn't used them for days at a time, and this was the first scouting mission they would be required for since Belgium. That seemed like weeks ago to Dan.

He watched as both men organised their equipment and rode away at low revs to maintain a lower noise profile. Shortly afterwards, Jack arrived with a fresh mug of coffee to relieve him.

"Blessings of God to you, friend," he said quietly in his broad Belfast accent, a perfect mimic of the same first words he had ever said to Dan.

"And to you, Jack. Thanks," he replied as he took the drink.

"You go on now and get some rest," Jack said as he climbed stiffly up on a wheel to reach the top of the vehicle. "I'll take it from here," he finished as he settled himself down with his favourite large pump-action shotgun across his knees.

At this stage, neither Dan nor Leah needed to find a quiet spot to sleep. They were both so tired that they climbed into the back of their armoured truck, wriggled their way into sleeping bags in full clothing and were unconscious in minutes. Neither stirred at all until the high-pitched engine note of the two-stroke Hondas cut into Dan's brain. He sat up, joints creaking and cracking as he moved, waking Leah as he did so. She sat up too, only far quicker and without the percussive fanfare brought on by age and a life of pushing physical limits, and both looked at their watches simultaneously.

They had slept for just over five hours, which was days short of what they needed but more than ample to carry on.

As they climbed out of the back of the truck, Dan cursed silently as he saw Henry duck back behind the larger of their vehicles only to reappear bearing two hot drinks.

Dan's annoyance, while exasperated by their tiredness, was becoming almost intolerable. The boy was obsessed with him. With her.

With both of them.

Henry wanted nothing more than for the pair of them to like him, just not the dog. Henry reckoned Ash still recalled what he tasted like and wasn't eager to repeat the incident.

A groan escaped Dan's mouth, and he was quietly chided by the girl.

"He's only trying to help," she said under her breath as the grinning boy strode purposefully towards them. "Don't be an arse!"

Having been left insufficient time to answer her before the excited arrival of their coffee, he turned a wan smile towards Henry and thanked him for the drink before walking away as slowly as he could bear to be polite. This had the added bonus of giving him a small snippet of awkward and forced conversation as the boy, complete with his wispy chin sprouting the fuzz of which he seemed pathetically proud, tried to engage Leah in some casual conversation.

"Don't be an arse!" He quietly mocked her in a whiny voice as he walked, earning a patented ears up, head cocked response from Ash, who had rushed to his side as soon as the door of the truck opened.

"Don't you start on me too," he told the perplexed dog.

Glancing back, he saw that Leah, in spite of what he thought, was interacting with Henry and wore the most curious look on her face as she brushed a strand of greasy and unruly hair behind her ear.

Good God, he thought, *she's actually flirting with him*. On reflection, it wasn't that unexpected. He was almost sixteen, she was nearing fourteen, and although they were either side of proper when it came to the age of consent, he guessed that Henry was her only real contemporary in the group. The thought of having to have "the talk" with her was more worrying than a firefight, but he was sure Marie could deal with that.

Marie.

As soon as he thought of her, he realised that he callously hadn't given her a single thought since he woke. Crucifying himself for being heartless and trying to blame the tiredness, he promised himself to see her as soon as he had spoken with the returning Rangers.

Flicking away the end of the cigarette as though it was the remnants of his guilt, he strode purposefully towards the resting motorbikes as the two dust-covered men recovered from time in the saddle.

Placing both hands on the small of his back and leaning back to push out his gut, Neil looked suddenly like a travel-stained Santa Claus. The ridiculous posture made Dan's face crack into a smile, which gave Neil a perfect opener.

"You'd do well to look happy, old boy," he said, greeting him cheerfully in his favourite go-to character: the Wing Commander. "Barracks ready for inspection!" he crowed with a mocking salute. Too tired to spar with Neil, Dan turned and raised an eyebrow to Mitch.

The soldier shrugged as though to imply that the entertainment wasn't that good, so he had no concerns with the channel being switched over.

"Campsite. Wooden buildings, compost toilets, geothermic eco stuff according to him." Mitch indicated Neil, who still grinned at Dan in character. "Set in a valley, thick woodland on two sides, topography is impossible to assault by vehicle and the main entrance is easily defended. If we were blocked in, we'd still have a hundred evac routes on foot."

The succinct report of the defensive capabilities of the site gave Dan little cause to complain. If Mitch said it was safe, then it was safe.

If Neil said it could sustain them temporarily, then he trusted that assessment too.

"How far?" Dan asked.

Sensing that the comedy act was no longer drawing a crowd, Neil answered him straight. "Hour on the bikes. Fairly easy roads."

Dan nodded. "Any other movement?" he asked, turning to Mitch.

"Nothing I've seen. A few deserted towns with no signs of life and what looks to be a fire burning out in the city," Mitch said.

"City?" Dan asked, looking around as though he would suddenly see something he hadn't noticed before.

"Dijon," Neil informed him. "The place is probably less than an hour southwest of it."

Squinting his eyes as though that would help him recall the geography, Dan felt as though they had just driven in circles around Europe for a week. They still had hundreds of miles to cover until they had a hope of getting to the south coast without making a straight run on the major roads.

Pushing that thought away, he thanked the two men and asked them to stow the bikes before taking a break.

"We move in one hour," he told them, eager to be in place before the sun began to set on another wasted day. He moved off, clicking his fingers out of autonomous habit and bringing the loping dog close to his leg. He walked along the convoy which seemed to have vomited people and equipment from everywhere he looked. He told the people to pack up their belongings, to be ready to move soon, and he did it wearing a relaxed smile and trying to exude the air of easy self-competence and reliability that they used to know.

He tried to recall the feelings of excitement, of adventure, of happiness he felt to be undertaking the journey they had followed him on. His smile grew as he made jokes with some, reassured others and wound his way circuitously to the large canvas-backed truck where the resting Marie was propped up on a throne of ration pack boxes padded out with coats and sleeping bags. She watched his approach as he climbed aboard and pointedly ignored Sera's presence; when those two were fully rested, she thought to herself, they could have a fight over the colour of grass.

He was followed, with a total lack of dignity, by Ash, who only gained the tail step of the truck on his second scrambling attempt.

Kneeling down at her side, he took her hand in his and stroked it as he looked up at her.

"You're so melodramatic!" she said, mocking him and looking over his shoulder to pat the arm of her makeshift seat and invite the dog to spring over the obstructions to settle down awkwardly at her left hand. Dan fought down the *Game of Thrones* reference burning on his tongue and let out a small laugh at her levity. Of everyone he had ever met, she was the only person to have never taken him seriously.

Many others had little or no respect for him, but her mocking was different; it was as though she knew the world was a terrible, dark place but she refused to let that pessimism infect her. She laughed at him whenever he tried to be serious, and when he tried to show concern, she mocked him further for overacting the part.

"How are you feeling?" he said to her, moving past being the butt of her joke.

"I fainted," she said seriously. "I didn't lose a kidney. I'm fine."

He smiled at her light-heartedness again and told her they had to pack up and move for maybe two hours at the most. From behind him, the protests started in full surround sound from Kate, Sera and two others who were watching the show, but Marie silenced them all with a raised hand to allow Dan to finish.

"Neil and Mitch have found somewhere we can rest up for a week. I want to be there before sundown."

"OK," she said simply. He rose and kissed her tenderly on the forehead, prompting a retching noise from her.

"Do your teeth before I see you next!" she said from behind the hand covering her mouth.

Backing away, he had to admit she had a point. Walking to the head of the convoy with Ash back at his heel, he looked to the dog.

"New low, eh boy?" he said to the dog, as though he expected a response.

"Yep," he said, as though the conversation were actually happening two ways. "It's definitely a new low when you can smell yourself."

~

Three hours later, the convoy halted a quarter of a mile back from the big wooden entrance under guard while Dan and Leah went forward on foot with four-legged backup. Trees and grass had overgrown what looked like an impressive entrance. It had the feel of one of those traditional carpentry places Dan had seen in an almost forgotten past: all wooden pegs, hand tools and no metal fixings.

The entrance was at the end of a wide track with steeply sloped banks on both sides as it entered into the bowl of a valley. Thick woodland ahead loomed menacingly, but Dan had that hunter's eye for terrain and knew it would serve well. He had been told that the stream running from high on his left went through the campsite and into a lake further down the green bowl of land they were in.

Daydreaming, he couldn't understand why this place, which must have been a prime spot for a settlement when such naturally occurring things mattered so much, had not grown into at least some grand residence. The answer was only hinted at when Leah pointed to a faded sign bearing a striking red logo. Unable to read or decipher the lettering, he could only assume that there was some lottery grant or historical trust money involved in preserving this place.

A cobbled courtyard opened up to become a kind of village square, and at the far end of it stood the single largest building. Stables, large lean-to sheds and a series of smaller buildings surrounded it. They seemed to have walked into an overgrown set from some medieval film, and the results could not have been better.

The majority of the buildings were weatherproof and dry, there was a central well on top of the running stream Dan could hear, and thoughts of the fresh game in the woodland made this place look like a haven in their backwards world without the modern accoutrements to which they had all become so debilitatingly reliant upon. Systematically, they worked through every building until taking a full perimeter, one half-sphere each, until they met at the site's furthest end where the stream ran downhill to the lake. Swinging the carbine behind his back, and seeming to signify to Leah that she could stand down, he took a packet of cigarettes from the battered pouch which had been custom-made and stitched onto the front of his vest.

Lighting up and inhaling deeply, he was transported back months to when he stood looking out over another lake with a young girl wearing brightly coloured clothing and making pretty notes with her new pens as she ate sweets.

"What do you think, then, kid?" he asked Leah.

She sighed, as though she too reminisced about the more simplistic past before she answered.

"Perfect location. Approach is easily ambushed but is the only vehicle access, emergency exits are situated *hyah*, *hyah* and *hyah*," she said in passable mockery of Neil impersonating an air hostess as she stuck out one hip and made gestures with her hands at the surrounding woodland before continuing. "Cut back some of the trees for better line of sight on the approach and we can sit tight here for weeks. The bonus, obviously, is that there are no fresh bodies to burn," she finished, finally letting him know they were both in mind of the same shared conversation.

"Yeah, but do you like it?" he asked with a smile.

"It'll do," she said, smiling back.

KICKING THE HABIT

For the last three days and nights, Steve had sat in his uncomfortable bed experiencing a maelstrom of emotions and sensations. His temperature never remained consistent; he raged from fever-like sweats to such deep cold that he felt as though his very bones were frozen.

The only consistent feeling was the agonising pain in his head and the sensation of having swallowed acid and having to feel it burn slowly through every part of him.

His reluctant nurse, Jan, spent most of the time with him, and although he seemed happy enough to talk in a quiet voice when spoken to, Steve was rarely in a lucid state to converse. The big South African just sat still and quiet, reading book after book.

His body rejected most of the food he was given, and as a result the drip had to stay in his arm. The only temporary reprieve was when he was given minute doses of opiates to ease the pain.

In truth, the injuries were no longer that severe, but the amount of morphine he had been given was way over the recommended dosage.

Steve was in withdrawal and suffering badly.

Jan knew this, and told him so, but Steve vehemently denied being addicted. He saw it as an insult, an affront to his character. He was a career military pilot, so how could he be an addict?

He pushed the thoughts away and lapsed back into a waking coma of pain and shivering.

Every day, he was half carried to the toilet block to clean himself and rid his skin of the dry film of sweat. His hands were still so unsteady that he allowed his constant shadow to trim the grey beard he had sprouted. He couldn't bear the thought of someone else holding a razor to his skin, so he left the short beard and accepted a close haircut to match. Wiping the condensation from the cold mirror, he saw his reflection again and the shock of his resemblance to a prisoner of war brought him low once again.

Small snippets of information kept coming to him about the others; they had been mostly separated and given work details among the other "protected" civilians. The camp seemed to have close to six or seven hundred people inside, and at least one in ten were wearing some form of uniform as a kind of semi-legitimate militia.

Ostensibly they were there to guard Richards's survivors, but the guards seemed mostly to be looking inwards, not for outside threats.

Jan worked him hard, never showing an ounce of sympathy for the pain he was in or the wretched feelings he had. Every time the physiotherapy he had to endure daily became too painful and he curled up in a foetal position, his nurse would berate him like a child and tell him he was weak. That he was giving up. That if he didn't want to get better, then there was no point in him surviving the helicopter crash.

As Steve lay back on his bed, out of breath and sweating through exertion of his weak and atrophied muscles, Jan sat close and asked him why he thought he survived.

"The crash?" he asked, confused by the change of direction.

"All of it. The sickness, the shit you went through after that, the crash. Why didn't you die at any point before now?" Jan asked seriously.

Unsure if the questions were rhetorical, Steve remained silent until the answers were given to him.

"Because you weren't meant to," came the eventual solution. "None of those times were your time, so there's still something important you need to do with your life, otherwise why did fate spare you?"

The concept of fate and faith being raised by the big, scarred man in front of him who seemed simultaneously capable of a destructive rage and providing genuine care threw him again and sent his mind into a tailspin that no pilot could have recovered from.

On his small walks around the immediate vicinity, he saw that the sprawling camp had been extended using buildings, shipping containers and some heavy-duty fencing. Guard posts had been erected at intervals and everything seemed to be running like clock-work. A mirthless smile appeared on Steve's face as he thought about Richards: this was the exact kind of order he wanted; the fact that it was achieved through fear and force wouldn't bother him, just so long as there was order.

Auschwitz was probably a very orderly place too, he thought soberingly.

As the days wore on and his strength and senses returned to him piecemeal, he began to orchestrate a plan.

Whether that plan would work yet, he had no idea. He only knew that he would not live under tyranny, and he owed it to everyone he knew, and those he didn't yet know, to free them from under Richards's blanket of fear and compliance.

He would take control of Camp Bloody Bravo, somehow, and by God he would turn it into what it should be.

Free.

Which meant that Richards had to go.

NATURE'S BOUNTY

Dan's happy band of adventurers settled in quickly, probably more to do with their eagerness to be stationary for more than a few hours than for any other reason.

Huts were claimed, beds hastily made and orders given to make the small settlement home for a short while.

Dan walked the perimeter again with Mitch, making mental preparations for some work they needed to do to increase their defences. Turning on Dan with red-ringed eyes, Mitch had clearly wound himself up to say something that Dan may not like.

Too tired to argue, and too trusting of Mitch to have to show dominance, he asked him what was on his mind.

"How long are we going to stay here?" he blurted out.

"Not sure," Dan replied. "A week?"

Mitch kicked at a rock and kept his eyes on the ground, making Dan feel like he disagreed with him but wasn't sure how to say what he wanted to.

"Just spit it out, man!" Dan said, although as kindly as he could manage.

"It needs to be longer," he snapped back. "Everyone is fucked, and not just the civvies but our blades too."

Dan had to smile at that: it had been a while since he'd heard someone refer to their fighting strength as blades. While Dan was inclined to agree, he sensed that there was more on Mitch's mind.

"So how long do we wait?" he asked gently. "A month? Two? By which time we'll be wading through shitty weather and snow trying to head south. We're already out of summertime, the nights are getting longer and the temperature drops every day. How long will we last on the road in winter, for fuck's sake?" he finished, more in exasperation than anger.

His voice had risen higher as he spoke, and realising that he had just inadvertently shouted Mitch down, he shrank himself back to his normal size and tried to put the anger and frustration back in its box.

"You're right," he said, by way of a weak apology, "but so am I. So what's the compromise?"

Brushing off the hostility and confrontation instantly, Mitch had his answer loaded and ready to fire. "Two weeks," he said. "Long enough to recoup, but not so long that people get comfortable and decide to live in a mud hut forever."

Fixing him with a look, Dan simply agreed. Dropping his cigarette end on the dirt and grinding his boot onto it, he walked away without another word.

Watching the conversation from a short distance away, two people emerged from their hiding places of minding their own business and made their way towards Mitch.

"Well?" asked Kate.

"Two weeks," Mitch replied, seeing Kate bite her lip and consider what they could achieve in that time.

"It'll have to do," said Neil, joining the small circle. "Any longer and Marie will be struggling, and I don't want to be carting her around when she starts looking really pregnant."

"In that case," Mitch said, turning his tired face to look at Neil, "I need your help getting a sentry post up."

Kate watched the two men walk away discussing the necessary building materials and let out a sigh which was somewhere between exhaustion and desperation.

Two weeks was more than enough to patch everyone up and get them properly rested, but delaying any longer would mean they may be stuck in medieval France for a whole winter.

Which would mean a death sentence for Marie and the baby. If that happened, Dan would fall apart.

If Dan fell apart, she had very little hope of any of them surviving to see another summer.

A day and a half later, things in their small village looked very different.

The vehicles had been carefully backed into the small square, with the tallest blocking the entrance and facing outwards. The main truck was too big to reverse fully inside, so it acted as an obstacle and a sentry post in one. A small shelter had been erected on the roof of the cab, with all the comforts required of a discerning night sentry: water heater, seat, high-powered rifle and snacks.

Kate had claimed a section of the main hall as a field hospital and laid out all her gear. Marie was propped up in the corner and instructed to do nothing but rest as every other member of the group, with no exceptions, was given a health check.

Dan tried to decline but was instructed that in no uncertain terms would he be exempt.

"Who's the highest authority on a warship?" Kate asked him when he told her he was fine.

The question caught him off guard, and he sensed that the logic of the conversation was already predicted so that he lost with whatever counter-argument he raised.

"The ship's doctor," he answered grudgingly.

"Exactly," Kate said, looking proud to have won but a little disappointed to have achieved victory without a fight.

"So, Captain," she said with heavy sarcasm, "sit your arse down and let me check you out!"

As she fussed over him, he asked her quietly about Marie. He had tried to ask the woman herself, only to be unceremoniously ejected from the hall so she could be violently sick.

"The morning sickness is crippling her, but it's supposed to be the worst around this time. She's starting to show more and I doubt that our little road trip has helped with that. She's dehydrated and tired, but I can fix that."

She stayed silent for a while as she calculated his heart rate with her fingers and a stethoscope.

"As for the long-term fix," she said when she had finished, "I'm afraid that's on you."

As if the burden was not already painfully apparent, the reminder sent Dan back out to his duties with a heavy heart. Pausing to light a cigarette in the crowded square, the smell of coffee touched something inside him and inspired him to hunt down the source until his need for caffeine was satisfied.

Much to his disappointment, the source rested with Henry. Having made his entrance, he could hardly ignore the boy and leave, so he accepted a cup and tried to play nice. Henry was tinkering with a wind-up radio in the desperate hope of finding something other than static. An excruciating few seconds of watching the boy turn the dial millimetre by millimetre threatened to shatter his pretence of being able to tolerate him. Unable to contain either his patience or his irrational temper any longer, Dan rose to leave.

As he began to walk away with Ash loping to flank him, the static broke, rewarding the boy's perseverance with a flash of garbled speech.

It was unintelligible, not spoken in English, but it was undoubtedly words.

Dan froze and spun back to the boy, who wore a look of such triumphant horror that he sparked both pride and an immense annoyance in the older man. Brushing away the latter, Dan strode back towards him with such purpose that Henry almost spilled from his seat on a log thinking that Dan may have finally cracked and would go for him again.

"What was the frequency?" Dan snapped at him.

Dumbstruck by the radio and Dan speaking to him, he simply opened and closed his mouth without a single word escaping.

"The frequency?" Dan said again, more patiently this time. "What was the frequency?"

Flustered, Henry picked up the radio, which still wavered between static and silence, and squinted at the dial.

"Just after six hundred," he stammered.

Spinning away, Dan scanned the faces of those people he could see looking for Neil. As much as he wanted to bawl his name, the panic that would cause in others was not worth the excitement, so he kept quiet. Eventually finding him close to the entrance, he told him what Henry had found.

"Could be a voice loop from before?" Neil offered by way of being a devil's advocate, only to reverse that opinion as he worked through the logic. "But nothing would still have power to be broadcasting without someone looking after it," he said, moving his hands as he thought through the possibilities. "If it was anything but static, it must be manned. Think about it, even if something had an indefinite power source like solar and was set to repeat a recorded loop, by now it would have needed cleaning or maintenance to keep going." He looked at Dan with excitement, not knowing that the two men had very different ideas.

"We need to hear what they're saying," Dan said. Just as Neil began to agree, Dan continued. "I want to know who they are, where they are and what their capabilities are. I need to know if they are a threat."

The disappointment on Neil's face was sadly evident. His friend, the person still alive that he had known for the longest time, the man capable of such heroic compassion and empathy for others, was broken.

Everywhere he looked, he saw danger. Every person they met was an invader to him. He understood that some of the paranoia, in fact most of it, was completely justifiable, but the sadness Neil felt for him then was incredible. Dan simply couldn't allow himself to think that there was anyone good left in the world.

Thinking how best to explain this to him, Neil gently offered an alternative suggestion. "Or we could find out what they're saying, where they are, who they are and try to understand why they're broadcasting a message," he said. "Remember when we left a message the first time? That brought us Leah…"

He left the last comment hanging heavily on Dan's conscience. The dirty face with its scruffy beard which was starting to show grey in patches looked up at him past the angry scar running down over his left eye.

Before he could ask, Neil anticipated and answered.

"We need a big metal aerial, somewhere up high." And when Dan opened his mouth to ask where, the older man simply pointed behind his shoulder to the hills in the distance. Sitting proudly on top was a string of large metal pylons.

"Climb up one of those, and I reckon you'll get the message."

Dan stared forlornly into the distance. He didn't know whether it was the prospect of heights or the risk of disappointment which twisted his insides more.

SUMMER HOLIDAY

The gear was packed, repacked and carefully placed into the Land Rover like jigsaw pieces to achieve the most efficient fit. Precious diesel was siphoned into the extra tank on the roof, and spare tyres were checked for pressure.

They could afford no more delays, unless they wanted to be testing the off-roader's ability to traverse a snow-covered continent.

Melissa was adamant that she was done running. Lexi suspected that she had made friends in the group who had convinced her to stay, but most of them curiously avoided the newcomers. Simon, by way of association she incorrectly assumed, was included in that avoidance.

Dressed in a mismatch of different colours now, both Paul and Lexi had found themselves forgoing their usual black attire. There seemed little point in continuing the trend anyway.

Chris remained sullen and hostile despite his usual nature, and Lexi suspected that the loss of Melissa was stinging him on a more personal level. She recalled the gossip of the house that the two spent a lot of time together on the farm after he and Ana split, but the relevance of that seemed insignificant now. Either way, having a grumpy adult in the back seat of an already cramped vehicle on a long journey asking if they were there yet seemed less than inviting.

Lexi asked Simon directly why he didn't seem to play much of a part in his own group, but the big man deftly turned the question away in such a manner that she was left even less sure of the answer. The most she could gather was that he seemed to be in charge before he met Dan, but then when he came back as the sole survivor, something changed. She couldn't be certain if it was the group's feelings towards him or Simon himself, but something had definitely changed.

If he was planning on joining them to escape, then that was OK with her; he was a capable and very reassuring man to have around. If he was joining them to cleanse some debt, then that gave her cause for concern.

Regardless of mood, and with almost no ceremony whatsoever, they rose early and squeezed into the truck to drive east without a word.

Lexi liked the Land Rover, but she could never understand how such a big vehicle could force a difficult choice: the driver had to either forgo using their right hand for much other than holding the wheel still, or wind down the window to allow elbow room. The choice between awkward steering and constant draught was an uneasy one to make, but Lexi, having the smallest frame by far, made her the best choice for driver. Paul sat behind her with a map on his knees and his rifle propped next to him, whereas Lexi placed her own on the dash. Simon sat in the passenger's seat with a shotgun between his knees, and Chris sat behind him, looking out of the window in silence.

That silence infected the cabin for most of the four hours it took them to reach the outskirts of the capital. From the large, encircling motorway which was usually at a standstill with too many cars all trying to get to the same place, they could see the haze of destruction resting above London where the imagined cloud of smog would be.

Without a word, they all stopped to stare at the brooding place like it was some mythical dark zone that they were forbidden to enter. Lexi saw Simon stifle an involuntary shudder: whether it was about his imagination at what horrors had happened there when it happened or whether it was the country dweller's inherent fear of built-up areas, she didn't know.

They drove on, weaving through more and more obstacles now as they pushed further into the population centres. As one, and without any words of caution, all four occupants became more alert now that they were feeling surrounded by more concrete than they were used to.

Perhaps it was a form of evolution, Lexi thought. Like wild animals instinctively knowing to watch the skies for predators, were they evolving to keep themselves safe through instinct? Or, more likely, were they simply all too aware of the risk they faced from other people?

Pushing onwards, and being forced to make a few minor detours, they reached their goal in the early afternoon.

To find a scene from a disaster movie.

FRENCH CONNECTION

After four days of living the natural lifestyle, moods had returned to something resembling normal. No longer were everyone's eyes rimmed red; no longer did people fall asleep mid-conversation through sheer exhaustion. Clothes were washed and dried, meals were taken in relative comfort and people tended to their small needs which weren't addressed when they were on the road.

Dan surveyed the quietly busy scene beneath him as he stood watch, feeling curiously like an outsider as he witnessed the normal goings-on of his group.

Thanks largely to the boxes of ration packs taken from storage in the military lines, their food needs were more than met, with each twenty-four-hour pack containing more calories than most of them needed in three days. They were designed to keep soldiers in the field fighting fit with maximum efficiency.

The novelty of the packs never seemed to wear off, and it seemed to Dan that every person he saw had a foil packet of something edible. Being more partial to having a sweet tooth, he had already emptied all the boiled sweets, nuts, dehydrated fruit and cereal bars from a half-dozen packs and crammed the treats into every available space in his personal kit. He could never stand being hungry, and said as much to Mitch who, was sitting beside him in the sentry post.

"Mr and Mrs Death's three little boys," Mitch said, looking at Dan to see if he was following the train of thought.

Smiling, he held up his hand and counted off one finger at a time as they both spoke in unison.

"Cold, Wet, and Bloody Hungry," they chorused before lapsing back into an amused, comfortable silence.

Mitch was there to take over mid-morning so Dan could no longer delay his venture to the mast. He was both dreading and avoiding it while simultaneously excited to know if others had built something as good as they had at home.

Home. He still thought of it as home, even though he'd come to realise that the chances of making it back there were on the slim side. His home, whether he could articulate it or not, was wherever Marie, Leah and Ash were. If that happened to be sitting on top of an army truck, eating vegetarian all-day breakfast from a foil packet and surrounded by what were effectively mud huts, then that was just fine.

Only it wasn't. If they didn't find answers to questions they barely understood within a few months, then nothing would be fine ever again.

"Right," he said, his back painfully cracking as he stood. "Back by sundown. ERV five miles down the road if the shit hits the fan. If I'm not back by morning, then come and rescue me."

He hardly needed to reiterate the instructions to Mitch on what to do in the event of something unexpected, but he felt better for saying it all the same. He had argued adamantly against taking Henry to the mast, despite it being his discovery initially, and opted to go alone, as he didn't want to take away another gun from their small camp. The motorbike should get him most of the way there, and as long as he didn't fall off, then he should easily be back before nightfall.

Climbing down to find Ash had pre-empted him and was waiting at his feet when he landed, he told him he had to stay with Leah today. He was rewarded with a concerned look of misunderstanding, which incidentally was the same look when the dog's hopes for food were raised, but he followed obediently all the same.

Finding her lounging on boxes of ration packs with her feet up and a nail file gently sculpting the tips of her fingers came as no great surprise, as Dan had come to accept that she was, after all, a girl.

Pointing first at Ash and then to Leah, he gave simple instructions.

"You, stay." Ash glanced once at Leah, then both looked back to Dan in unison. "And keep the dog with you. I'll be back before dark," he said as he turned to leave.

"Hilarious as ever," came the muttered sarcasm aimed at the back of his head.

Neil had already prepared a bike for him, and he said goodbye to Marie, who mildly scolded him for being soppy. A hint of seriousness crept into her voice, edged with concern, as she asked him, "Are we going to catch a break soon?"

Smiling to reassure her, he kissed her and promised they would. Soon.

He took the wind-up radio and the length of wire which Neil had given him instructions on how to use, and he set off at an easy pace down the road.

Maybe the relaxed atmosphere of being stationary for recuperation dulled his senses slightly, but instead of his usual paranoid alertness, he allowed himself to enjoy the ride. He was in an area of soft, green, rolling hills, which in the absence of people was truly beautiful.

By midday, he had reached the nearest piece of road to the high bluff where the metal museum piece stood proudly. As he nursed the bike carefully through the overgrown grass up the slope, he wondered absentmindedly how long it would stand before nature showed its slow-moving might and reduce it back to the raw materials from which it was made. A long time, he guessed, but still it was an inevitability that every trace of their feats of engineering would become relics. Maybe one day people would look at the remnants of the Seven Wonders and seek answers in ancient texts about their origins.

That musing killed his blissful mood as the thought of human survival hit him hard in the gut. He concentrated on pushing on, of reaching this goal so he could move on to the next. Have something to fix, have somewhere to be, have a reason to get up in the morning and live. That's how he had lived his life before it all went to shit, and he didn't like to admit that he preferred it now to how it used to be.

Marie's words echoed back to him as he struggled higher still: "You were broken before all this happened, so it fixed you in a way. It gave you a purpose again." He didn't know if it made him a bad person or not, nor did he really give it enough thought to care, but he had enjoyed the last months more than most of the years before.

No point in dwelling on it, he told himself; it was what it was, and he had a job to do.

Eventually, the bike would go no further through the long grass, and after he had turned off the engine, which had stalled, and pulled all of the foliage from between the spokes of the front wheel, he rested the bike down and trudged the last part on foot.

Neil's instructions were simple: stick the wire in the radio and put the other part as high up as he could reach.

Neil didn't know of Dan's fear of heights, or his healthy respect for the "force of gravity," as he preferred to call it, but the wire he had given him was thirty feet if it was an inch.

"Thanks, Neil, you bastard," Dan complained to himself. Bracing one foot into a join of two heavy pieces of metal, he began to climb hand over hand until he reached the ring of sharp spikes and barbed wire designed to stop foolish people attempting to scale the pylon.

Hanging on tightly, he looped the end of the wire, which he had tucked in the top of his vest, over the spikes a few times before casting the rest down to the ground.

Neil had sounded confident when he told Dan this, but now that Dan was the one perched precariously twenty feet from the ground, he suddenly had doubts. Shaking, inch by inch, Dan returned himself to his natural state of having both feet on the ground.

Eager to be away from the scary high thing, Dan picked up the radio and pulled back the heavy-duty sticky tape attached to the back of it so he could force the wire into the aerial socket. Taping it back into place, he spun the winding handle a dozen times and settled down to fine-tune the dial.

Static. He carried on turning the dial millimetre by millimetre.

At 603.5 kilohertz medium wave, the static broke and he could hear a faint voice. Without doubt, a human voice was broadcasting on the other end of that frequency somewhere. In his excitement to hear the words, he held the speaker next to his ear until it occurred to him to turn up the volume. He cranked it to eleven and listened.

As Neil suspected, it was a looped recording, but that didn't put Dan off, as the chances of something automated still broadcasting after all that time was impossibly small. The words were coming through, mostly, but that wasn't the problem.

Of all the skills he had, mastery of the French language was not among them.

In fact, of all their group, none of them spoke French other than bits and pieces forced into their brains from their school years, which for most were a distant past.

As best as he could, Dan wrote down the message as he listened to the words loop over and over.

He wrote down everything he could make out, and when he looked at his notes, it seemed to be a puzzle calling to him, pleading for him to understand and mocking his ignorance.

"...tous les survivants. Nous...sécurité...et la famille. Notre...imprenable et a résisté...générations. Nous som...Nous viv...la vie. Nous...Sanctuaire. Fort...Sud."

Sitting back and lighting a cigarette, he began to logically unwind the clues on his paper.

"Survivants is survivors?" he said aloud to himself as he sketched a guessed translation next to each word. "Security, obviously," he muttered as he worked on. After five minutes, he read his best estimation of the message back to himself.

"Survivors. Security. Family. Impregnable. Resist. Generations. Life? Sanctuary. Fort. South." With a pleased smile, he read his notes aloud once more, then his elation evaporated.

As pleased as he was at having figured out a few words of French, he still had little or no clue what the message actually meant.

It could be a call to survivors offering sanctuary.

It could be a threat to outsiders to stay away.

It could be a bloody advertising campaign miraculously still playing so many months after the store closed down permanently.

Either way, it made little difference because he had no indication of where the damned place was. He had no idea how far radio waves could travel, but at a guess it must be hundreds of miles, which narrowed it down to, well, France.

Deflated, he packed up the radio and decided to leave the makeshift aerial booster in situ. He was convinced it had done nothing to help anyway.

Hoping that someone else could piece together more than he could, he stowed his notepad and heaved his small pack back on to retrieve his bike and return to the others.

THE UNDERGROUND MOVEMENT

As Steve gained more strength, his daily excursions around the camp became longer and reached further. He was being helped along on his crutches and twice saw people he knew; one didn't see him, he was sure, and the other just looked terrified at the guard next to her and turned away.

He couldn't remember her name but thought she worked on the gardens. Maybe she was from the group they rescued from the shipping containers. Maybe she wasn't. His memory was terrible since the crash; the trauma, being in and out of consciousness for days on end and his subsequent reliance on opiates had hazed the past badly for him.

He would poke fun at Dan for not learning all the names of the people they lived with, knowing that it bugged him and made him feel a little shallow, but now he was faced with the same prospect. There was only so much room inside a person's head, and right now his was too messed up to recall the small details. Looking around at the way everyone moved in small groups, some escorted by armed soldiers, made him mindful that this was not a safe place. This was hostile territory. He was living behind enemy lines and he had to portray no threat to them.

Concentrating on appearing weak while he exercised, he started to take note of everything he saw. Within a week, he had almost a half square mile mentally mapped out, all the while asking innocuous questions about which buildings were used for what purpose. He was sure to keep his information gathering as innocent as possible; although he was certain of Jan's lack of loyalty to the cause, they were always followed by at least one armed guard.

For his own safety, obviously.

"Am I going to get moved back into the normal population?" he asked his nurse, who was painfully moving his leg during a therapy session.

"I haven't been told anything," he answered, as he often did when Steve questioned him about the camp. Steve was learning to take the man literally, and phrase his questions as such.

"What were you told when you were assigned to fix me up?" he phrased deliberately.

"To fix you up," came the gruff answer, followed by a smile touching the corners of his mouth at his own humour. A conversation with Jan was like a game of chess.

Thinking about it, Jan saw no harm in elaborating on his answer.

"Fix you up. Don't tell you anything. Don't let you wander off," he said simply. "And I have to report on your progress," he finished, putting a sarcastic emphasis on the last word.

"My progress?" Steve asked innocently.

"Yep," came the reply before he paused to push on Steve's leg with more effort, earning the pilot a stab of pain. "He wants to know what you are saying about him."

"He" was obviously Richards, and from the way Jan said it, he was clearly no friend to the South African. The arrogance and insecurity of Richards would be laughable, if only he didn't have a small army to impose his will on others. Steve was certain that, if left unchallenged, Richards would soon drop the pretence and announce himself as dictator. In any normal society, not that things were normal anywhere nowadays, declaration of martial law was seen as extreme. It was to admit that the bounds of acceptable society, of decent human behaviour, had broken down and that a crushing show of force was required to re-establish those boundaries.

The use of an armed people's militia, in Steve's opinion, was now a definite must for any group, but the militarisation of the population and the classifications of type of worker just felt horribly oppressive.

It was an occupation, he decided. That was the best way to describe the sombre feeling in the camp. They were protected, sheltered and fed, but they weren't free.

Given the choice, he believed that most people would choose risk and hunger if the price for them was their own liberty. Bringing himself back to the moment, he pressed his advantage and directly asked Jan his opinion on Richards.

Staring blankly back at him, giving nothing away, Steve didn't know whether he would answer or run straight to the man himself to report.

"The man's an arsehole," Jan said simply with a shrug, as though his opinion mattered little.

Relief washed over Steve; without this man onside, he had no hope of gaining any further assistance.

"He makes lots of pretty speeches about protecting people, but everyone is only here because he commands more guns." Jan leaned closer now, dropping his voice further. "I was happy before he turned up, and three of my friends died before we all gave up and all lined up like sheep to be told where to go and what to do."

He leaned back, as though the conspiracy could be detected through the walls, before adding, "So yeah, I'd like to see him gone, but I don't see how that's going to happen."

Steve also leaned back, although slowly to avoid aggravating his battered body, before responding. "Information is the key," he said. "Know your enemy," he quoted, waiting for agreement.

"Know your enemy, and learn about his favourite sport," Jan said with a smile.

Steve frowned, earning a rare chuckle from his companion.

"It's a quote from *The Art of War*," Steve said, embarrassed at having to explain his jest.

"I know," replied Jan with a broad smile. "You were quoting Sun Tzu, but I was quoting Nelson Mandela. And I think the man might've got this right too."

Totally confused now, Steve sat and listened as it was explained to him. When he finally understood, he saw that the sport approach might be the best but possibly the riskiest idea he'd heard in a long time.

LE TUNNEL SOUS LE MANCHE

Nobody spoke much as they rolled at a steady speed along the deserted and badly overgrown motorways of the desolate southeast of England. Forced to travel carefully down the middle of the three concrete lanes, the tall weeds sprouting from the central reservation occasionally brushed against their offside windows, just as the encroaching treeline of the nearside forced them away from the hard shoulder. Sporadic clusters of long-abandoned wrecks littered the grey and green monotony, giving brief pauses as they assessed the potential dangers before pushing through.

Ordinarily, the journey would have taken them half a day without having to compete for space on Britain's overcrowded roads, but having to be ever alert to the danger of ambush as well as vehicle-killing potholes caused by the weather and a total lack of repairs made that trek significantly more ponderous.

Every obstacle forced them to stop and watch as they defended themselves all around to any attack, then they would gingerly press on until the torturous sound of off-road tyres complaining over pitted concrete bore into their brains. At that pace, they eventually turned off the bigger roads and into the once-busy cross-Channel train terminal.

"I remember this place." Lexi spoke wistfully from the front passenger's seat. "My dad drove us to France years ago. It didn't look like this, though," she said, indicating the ruin and disrepair of the place which once saw thousands of cars making the international crossing every day.

Nobody answered. Not through impoliteness, but more from the air of rhetoric with which she made the distant recollection. People rarely spoke about life before; it was just easier not to think about it.

More cars were abandoned here, the filthy insides of the windows an indication of a once-living cargo. They drove on past, leaving the forgotten souls undisturbed. Not having brightly lit arrows to follow and yellow-vested staff to guide their path, finding the tunnel entrance took time. Driving slowly down a long concrete ramp, a scene of such chaos was unveiled that all four occupants of the car were struck open-mouthed at the carnage which lay below them.

It seemed that one last train had arrived from the continent.

One ill-fated locomotive had seared through the signs bidding them Bienvenue and without a coherent driver to slow their progress had careened straight through the terminal and collapsed in a concertina effect straight into the very end of the lines. Instantly derailed, and forced along by the thousands of tonnes of freight and passenger cars, the train had struck the thick walls and seemingly imploded. Remains of cars were spilled grotesquely across a wide area as the occupants of the train who had been sitting in their vehicles were spewed violently out, and the four looking on could only begin to imagine the horror of such a crash for anyone left alive.

Simon's thoughts turned to the possibility of any survivors. Not from the crash – that seemed perversely unlikely – but for anyone immune to the… Whatever it was, they would have surely known what was coming. Would have known that they were in for a brutal ending. Putting himself in that situation, he wondered if he would feel some small amusement at the irony of such a final chapter.

Looking at the wreckage once more, he decided that he probably wouldn't.

Finding their way onto the tracks without suffering a six-foot drop from the platform took much longer, but eventually they were bouncing uncomfortably along the gravelled tracks towards the looming black hole in front of them.

Not one word was spoken until the light in the cabin was snuffed out instantly as they went down the slight incline into subterranean uncertainty. With just a strained sigh from Paul, they began their crossing.

WHILE YOU WERE GONE...

Two hours after she watched Dan ride away looking like an overgrown child on a bike too small for him, Leah was walking the perimeter of their temporary camp for want of anything better to do.

She told herself it was training, that she was learning to work as a pair with Ash just as Dan did, but if she was honest with herself, she was actually playing. She shouldn't be playing though, she told herself; that was for kids, and she didn't have the luxury of playing anymore.

Still, training was allowed to be enjoyable, wasn't it?

She took cover behind a large tree, peered around and waved Ash off to her right, watching out of the corner of her eye as the big, grey dog slunk low and silent across the ground. Moving position again, she gave a single low whistle to call him to her side. Within seconds he joined her, nudging her leg once to let her know he was there. She had barely heard him move until he was close. Repeating this pattern, they moved deeper into the woodland than she had ventured before, and just as she became aware of that fact, a flash of movement ahead snatched her attention.

Sinking low and raising the gun for real, she flicked the fire selector to semiautomatic. Sensing that the mood had changed, Ash dropped into a crouch and sniffed the air. Realising that the wind was blowing from directly behind her, she knew how they had moved so close to something undetected. Silent and downwind, whatever had moved was once again imperceptible.

Wait, she told herself. It was most probably just an animal, but the feeling in her gut made her more cautious. Creeping forward as quietly as possible, she noticed a slight movement ahead again, accompanied instantly by a low growl from beside her. She sank lower, holding out a hand to quiet the dog, and watched.

In a small clearing, maybe fifty paces ahead through the trees, she saw colours. Not the autumn colours of woodland, not the warm yellowing of the leaves or the vibrant reds nature treated them to every year, but something distinctly and unnervingly man-made.

Holding her breath, she turned her head slightly from side to side to look for a better vantage point. Seeing a fallen log to her left, she crept slowly back from the more exposed bluff she was on and sank low to watch after setting Ash down to lie still. Wishing she could take credit for her four-legged companion's skills, she marvelled at how he stared intently towards the possible threat without making another sound.

Slowly, moving every muscle with infinite care, she eased the carbine's sight up to her eye and began to scan the woodland. After a few seconds, she found the source of the unnatural colour and let the rest of the scene come into focus. Sitting still on a fallen tree not dissimilar to her own hiding spot was a man. A bearded man wearing green and brown, as though he wanted to blend in, but the woolly hat on his head bore a red and yellow emblem. That was the flash of colour she had seen when the man turned his head.

He seemed unconcerned, like he hadn't realised he was being watched, so Leah was happy to stay and see how things panned out.

She was due on watch in an hour, so if she wasn't back in time, then all kinds of merry hell would be raised in camp.

After another minute of watching, she was glad of her patience. In the foreground of her scope, much closer than the man she was watching, another person dressed in drag clothing shifted their position as they leaned against a tree. Stifling a gasp in her throat, she forced herself to be calm, as he was close enough to hear her. Behind her, Ash still stared intently ahead, not that she could turn to look, but hadn't made a single sound.

Whoever these two people were, they were being very quiet for a reason. Slowly inching herself away from the log, she turned her head to look in the direction she had come from. She saw nothing to concern her, but nonetheless made sure that her escape route was clear to the best of her knowledge.

Shuffling back centimetre by centimetre, her body shook with the effort of being quiet even when she desperately needed to open up her lungs and breathe deeply. Judging that she had moved enough, she rose slowly and walked as carefully as she could, nodding for Ash to follow. Dropping onto slightly lower ground, she reckoned she had put enough distance between them and quickened her pace. Another hundred paces and her nerve broke; she sped up into a run as fast as her own safety would allow across broken ground littered with tree roots. Ash kept pace effortlessly as she burst into the camp to find most people already assembled by the gates.

There was a visitor.

Neil was on watch when the lone wanderer came into his sight. Raising a quiet alarm resulted in him being joined by Mitch only seconds later as both watched the approaching figure through telescopic sights.

By the build and the pinch of the waistline above the hips, Neil guessed that the unexpected visitor was female, and by all indications from the silhouette before him, nicely put together at that. She walked steadily, not too fast or too slow, with her arms out to the sides. As she came closer, Mitch spoke to him without raising his eye from the rifle.

"Female. Mid-thirties," he stated.

Neil could see that well enough for himself. She was wearing tight jeans and a T-shirt which didn't quite meet the leather belt she wore.

At a hundred paces, just before Mitch was about to issue a challenge, she stopped. Keeping her arms out to her sides, she performed a slow circle, showing the watching sentries that she was unarmed. Turning around a second time for good luck, she continued her methodical approach to the gates.

Standing and slowly loading a round into the chamber of his rifle, Mitch watched as the metallic sounds echoed down to her. The message was clear: she had come far enough.

"Bonjour. Je suis Christine," she called out in a curiously deep voice for such a slim woman.

Mitch's language skills were limited to only English and foul, but thought he recognised enough to believe that the woman had just said hello and was called Christine.

Happy with his cultured and very metropolitan experience, he jumped down to further the international working relationship by searching her at gunpoint. She complied readily enough, although she exuded an air of boredom as she responded to the sign language and grunted orders from Mitch.

Neil watched on, part mesmerised by the appearance of the woman who he would describe as striking more than attractive, and part worried about an encounter with another group. His experience of others over the last in recent history had left him cynical at best.

When Mitch was satisfied that the woman really was unarmed, he lowered his weapon and asked her what she wanted. As a typical Brit abroad, he was sure to speak loudly and slowly, as though that would aid her understanding.

She looked at him, her eyes boring through him and making him feel distinctly uncomfortable. There was something of a feline manner about the way she looked at him. The way she moved made him mindful of something predatory, and he decided that he didn't trust her.

"What do you want?" he said again, loud and slow.

"Talk?" she said with a heavy accent, unsure of the word.

She shrugged and rattled off a sentence in rapid-fire French, never taking her eyes off him or dropping the slightly amused look that a cat would give a mouse.

She tried again, pointing at Mitch.

"Français?" she said, mimicking his unintentionally condescending tone. Exasperated by the lack of understanding, she shrugged and dropped her arms to her sides petulantly.

"I come again," she said as she turned and walked away, "in English."

They could only watch as her hips snaked away down the long approach road. At that point, both men were snapped out of their voyeurism by a shout from inside the camp. Mitch ran back inside to see Leah jogging into the square.

"Two men in the woods," she said succinctly, barely out of breath, "just sitting still."

Ash sat obediently and looked up at the pair, unsure if the conversation would turn to him with praise. His head switched from soldier to teenager as though he was watching a tennis match as they took turns to speak.

"We've just had a woman turn up here," he told the girl. "She didn't speak English and just left. Too much of a coincidence that they aren't together."

Questions were fired from both sides, questioning whether the waiting men in the woods were armed, and Leah gave her responses before asking her own questions about the woman. All around them a buzz of excitement was growing as the others gossiped about what they had heard and what it could mean.

Leah became very aware of the small crowd gathering, and she twitched her head for Mitch to walk away with her.

"So what do we do?" she asked in a hushed tone when out of earshot of the others.

"Nothing until Dan gets back," Mitch replied dutifully, "but we need to prep. Two-minute drill?" he asked her with eyebrows raised.

"Two-minute drill. Yes," she replied after a moment's thought. This was something they had worked on with the whole group. When instructed, they were all to be ready to leave within two minutes. That meant that everything they weren't immediately using was to be packed up and ready to go at any time. It meant sleeping with your boots on. It meant raising the panic levels considerably, but it reduced the chances of them being caught with their collective trousers down.

Orders were given, extra guards posted and the group busied themselves packing all their gear away. Just as Leah was preparing to lay some noise traps in the woods with Jimmy, the sound of a motorbike engine pierced the sky.

THE ENEMY WITHIN

Eventually, Steve was summoned to see the major.

He instantly swallowed his involuntary scoff at the self-awarded promotion in a hierarchy which no longer held any semblance of credibility. He had no legitimate lieutenants or captains, nor did he answer to any colonels or generals. He was a self-styled military dictator, and no floral display of humility or service could hide that fact.

Still, Steve thought, *play along*. Play the weakling, don't be a threat, and keep your head down. If Richards saw him as a broken and beaten man, then he could not be forced to play a role in the subjugation of the occupied citizens. Could not be bullied or threatened into trying to fly again, not that he had any hopes of recovering the strength required to do so.

He had to appear weak, and although he had been preparing for this summons for days now, he still made a show of seeming flustered and confused. Although his wits were restored, he knew that his body was not. He couldn't hope to fight his way out of an ambush conducted by babies firing water pistols at this point, and he had to show the world for all he was worth that he was finished.

To allow even a flash of his inner fire to show through his eyes could spell his death, and if he died then his hopes for realising the plan he was hatching would die with him.

He shook. He twitched as he spoke and seemed to lose his focus. He seemed racked by sudden pains in his head and body and he could barely walk unaided. If Richards saw him as just a half-soaked cripple, then he would not try to use him and would not need to kill him.

He had to act it out perfectly.

The guard who had brought the summons was pre-empted by the news which was brought by a runner to the window at the back of his damp and breezy room. Jan's eyes shot up and fixed on Steve as he heard the gentle knock, knock, knock at the window before the unknown courier vanished into the sprawling camp. The agreed signal, whispered among the underground rebels over mealtimes, that Richards was planning to bring Steve to him.

The two nodded to each other, both aware of what they had to do now. Steve lay back and half curled up, feigning the pains that racked him as his body cried out for more morphine. Jan sat in the chair and silently ignored his pretend pain. Moments later, the door opened without warning and an armed man strode in. He had the look of a soldier in that he carried a rifle and wore a green camouflage uniform shirt and trousers, but the ill-disciplined and wild look he wore showed no signs of training. This man wanted to be on the winning side, and he enjoyed the power it afforded him over others. Had he been living somewhere else when it happened, then he would have become a follower of the King of Wales or Bronson. He was a bully, nothing more.

"Get up," he growled at Steve, who only responded with a whimper and curled up into a tighter ball. "The major wants to see you. Now!"

He offered no more words, merely glared at Jan until, with an annoyed sigh, he carefully folded the page in the book he was reading and placed it down before getting up and manhandling Steve upright. He was sure to treat him without any obvious sign of care or respect, like he was just doing the job he was given by watching over the sick man until he was told to do something else.

"On your feet, you bastard," Jan grumbled without any real malice as he forced Steve up into a sitting position, bringing him his crutches. Still he had to half hold him as he made his slow progress in leaving the cabin. Jan was sure to wrap him in an extra blanket to show just how much he felt the cold even though the temperature of early autumn was still warm. All part of the act.

Twice Steve feigned a stumble, and twice he had to be helped back up to continue on his way to the meeting.

Richards was not a man who liked to be kept waiting, and every minute Steve wasted getting there was likely to be a minute less spent in the company of the man, as he no doubt had a schedule he intended to stick to.

Eventually, he found himself at the bottom of the stone steps which were originally a library or museum, he guessed, the top of which sported a sandbagged embrasure complete with crew-served machine gun. Whatever the steps once led to, they were now the way into the headquarters of the camp commander. Already, Steve had heard reference made to Richards as "The Commander" as much as people called him "Major", and he guessed this distinction was one that the man would happily allow, as it afforded him the highest rank in people's eyes.

There was no higher power than him: that was what the message said loud and clear.

Sweating and exhausted from making the short journey seem infinitely more difficult than it truly was, Steve collapsed onto a hard wooden bench where he was told to wait. His chest heaved to recover the expended energy, and although he had pretended to be physically broken, he had to admit to himself that the truth was not a quantum leap away from the imagination.

Heavy, dark oak double doors which stretched halfway to the tall ceiling were thrown open, and out strode the magnanimous Major Richards, resplendent in his uniformed glory and flanked by his ever-present personal guard. This personal guard, if met under different circumstances, would raise hilarity of epic proportions. Dressed in camouflage as all the other "troops", these men stood out because they wore their combat trousers tucked into high boots, sported a bright red sash tied about their right arms and wore full-face balaclavas like terrorists filming a propaganda video. Maybe next they planned some thunderbolts on their collars.

Again, Steve had to fight to keep a laugh inside at the stupidity of how seriously this man took himself.

All comedy aside, he wondered just how hard a job it would be to overthrow this dictator; heavy machine guns guarding his head-quarters against the general populace as well as anonymous guards flanking his every step indicated a man who felt threatened. A man who felt comfortable and safe would likely surround himself with beautiful female assistants, not faceless armed men.

Forcing his head back into the game, Steve concentrated on tak-ing in every detail he could while acting like a broken man who offered no threat. With a glance at the guard who had summoned him, Richards nodded into the office with his chin and walked back inside after offering a single withering glance at the man he once thought would be his right-hand man.

Sitting behind his desk and producing a bottle with two crystal glasses, he was blithely unaware that he had tried the same forced camaraderie with Steve before. It had failed then too.

Pouring two ungenerous measures into the glasses as Steve was dumped unforgivingly into the chair opposite, he slid one over to him without a word. Playing the character well, Steve reached for the glass with a shaking hand and drank desperately as though he sought any temporary reprieve from the pain he felt. Coughing and choking on the fierce liquid, he wiped his mouth and leaned back in the chair, waiting.

Richards sipped his own drink and then swirled the contents in small circular motions as he looked intensely at the bottom of the glass. He stopped and looked directly at Steve.

"You caused a great deal of disappointment," he said icily, "not that any of it matters any more." He held eye contact with Steve a second past it feeling uncomfortable.

Smiling his false smile, he rose from his seat and waved a regal glass-filled hand at the window and the sprawling population centre spilling out as far as the eye could see.

"We've accomplished a great deal without your help and you should feel lucky; if you had done what you did now instead of then, it could be viewed as treason. The punishment for treason is death."

Steve's eyes widened at the revelation. The man had casually re-introduced capital punishment, demonstrating that he held the power of life and death and he wielded that power over the people like a spoilt child with a stick.

Satisfied that he had elicited a reaction of fear which he misread in Steve's expression, he went on with a well-rehearsed speech about their achievements in rescuing people and the protection he offered the world now. His vitriol extended deep into his own visions for a strong, united future.

The sheer depths of the man's depravity were becoming clear to Steve. He was the worst kind of lunatic alive.

A fanatic.

A powerful man so consumed by his own ideas that he would never be able to see how hated, how power-hungry and crazed he had become. He had brought back the death penalty to a desperately depleted population with no way of knowing if the human race could be propagated. He ruled with fear and violence to force people, who previously counted themselves as free and lucky, to work and fortify his compound. He put them to work in the fields farming to feed his growing army. He treated disobedience as treason. There was nothing more dangerous, Steve thought, than a man with power over others who wholly believed that he was the only one with the foresight to shape the future.

Finishing his podium speech, Richards sat down in his chair still wearing his ridiculous mask of the benevolent master. He saw Steve looking at him in horror, and his own ego made him interpret that as pure fear.

And why shouldn't this man feel fear? He stole from him. He made him look foolish and weak. He disappointed him.

Still, it wasn't hard to find him. Who else was flying around in a helicopter? It took only a few months for his scouts to report back with the location of their home, a prison of all ghastly places, and after that it was a simple matter to send in his best spies and then arrive in overwhelming force and take it all away from him.

Those he had selected for questioning had yielded a variety of different information; the fact that their leader and twenty others had left a short time before and not returned irked him considerably. He told himself he would have liked to meet this Dan character, to see if he stood up to all the things he had heard about him. If the stories were true, then this was a man who would surely see his vision of a united future. He would even have been worthy of a high-ranking position, which would obviously have helped integrate the rest of the group under his rule.

If he objected, or lacked the foresight to join him, then the virtuous opponent would have made a fine adversary and his eventual execution would have the same effect on the dissident members of his flock.

He sipped his drink again, staring coldly at the man who had embarrassed him once.

"Luckily for you, I'm feeling generous," he said, leaning back and half expecting thanks. "Besides, executing an unwell man would hardly offer much entertainment. Now begone! I'm tired of your company."

A nod was raised to one of the balaclava-clad guards and Steve was aggressively hoisted from his seat and sent back out into the hallway, where Richards's voice echoed out to him.

"Rest assured, I'll want to speak to you again when you are sufficiently healed. Everyone must earn their keep here."

Being so unceremoniously bundled from the grand office offered him a snapshot of a desk he had not seen when he entered. Behind the ornate wood, he saw a young man so elegantly groomed that he seemed almost feminine. The immaculately coiffed hair couldn't hide the red-ringed eyes which burned intensely. Another strand to the unfolding scheme fell into place for Steve at that moment.

The waiting guards chivvied him and Jan back to their isolation in silence. When he collapsed breathlessly onto his bed, he grabbed the nurse's arm and held tight.

"I promise you one thing," he said through gritted teeth, "that madman has to die."

PRIORITIES

It was unfair for Dan to have implied any failing in the others. In fact, after he had calmed down from hearing the news, he recognised that he would have done exactly as they had done.

Everything except let the woman leave.

Now they had an unknown group in the area, with no communication, who obviously had knowledge of the ground and some form of skill set. He would have liked to ask the woman himself, probably loudly and slowly in English, but he couldn't because they had simply let her go.

Recognising that he might have caused some offence by his reaction, he proceeded to give a few orders which he was certain would have been pre-empted.

"Put everyone on two-minute drills," he instructed his small council of advisors.

"Done," said Mitch.

"And double the guard," Dan said.

"Done," said Mitch again.

"The woods," he tried. "Guards posted at the rear?"

"Done," chimed in Leah, "and Jimmy's put up some noise traps with string and tin cans."

Good, Dan thought. They had done everything he would have done and they had done it quickly. Allowing them to feel proud of themselves for having performed the tasks before being told would lift their spirits, he knew. It was as close as he could come at the time to giving praise, but he was just too damned fearful of others. He felt too vulnerable.

"Did you get anything from the radio?" Neil asked him.

Digging into a pouch on the front of his vest for the pad of paper he had used caused a flurry of activity as Ash leapt up from his resting spot thinking that something edible was being produced. Seeing it was just a piece of paper, he settled back down to wait for the next opportunity.

As he read his own rough translations aloud, the others listened intently.

"Survivors. Security. Family. Impregnable. Resist. Generations. Life? Sanctuary. Fort. South."

Silence greeted him. Followed by a flurry of questions, none of which he could hear clearly as all the others were speaking. Holding up both hands to ward off the storm, he answered them all at once.

"I don't know what it means, I don't know where it is and I didn't get it all. It could be a warning to stay away, it could be an invitation to join them or it could lead to nothing. Right now, we need to focus on the immediate and worry about this afterwards. Leah, Neil, Mitch, with me, please."

With that, he walked out of the hut and into the square. His chosen companions knew him well enough by this point to wait until he had lit a cigarette before asking anything else.

"If I'm being honest with myself, the message sounds hopeful." He let that sink in and looked at the three pairs of eyes in front of him before he went on. "But the main problem is that we don't have a clue where this place is until we get a stronger signal; it says 'south' and that's the direction we need to go. The problem with getting a stronger signal is that one of us has to travel at least a day away from here to try again, and now that we have company, then that seems unlikely."

"I'll go," said Neil, launching into a defence before the challenges were made. "Look, you three are soldiers and I'm an old git who fixes engines. You're needed here more than I am right now."

"No," said Dan. "Thank you, mate, but that's exactly the reason you need to be with the group. I'll go, but not until we've figured out what that woman wants."

Mitch's face coloured slightly as he instantly regretted his adolescent description of the visitor to Dan.

"So what? We just wait for them to come back?" Leah asked, annoyed at the prospect of inaction.

"Yes," said Dan, almost challenging her to push back.

"Fine," she said, conveying anything but "fine" with her tone and glancing at her watch and walking away. "I'm due on watch."

"Ah, they grow up so fast," Mitch said sarcastically as she stomped away.

"They do when you give them an automatic rifle when they turn thirteen," Dan replied as he stamped out his cigarette and turned towards the woods.

After the next five days spent on high alert expecting some form of attack, nerves began to fray once again. Their soldiers were becoming exhausted again having to do double the hours as sentries.

As Dan sat with Marie, who never missed an opportunity to point out his lack of daily washing, she poked playfully at the scraggy mess of beard where it was turning white. She was trying to lighten his mood, and although it wasn't overtly working, at least she was distracting him from his brooding thoughts for a while.

He was brooding, even more so when he saw that she was showing now. A noticeable bump swelled her belly, the physical manifestation of the very reason they started out on this fool's errand at all.

He had to make a decision.

Marie seemed to sense this too, and giving up on her attempts to annoy him into smiling, she told him what he was thinking.

"It's been almost a week and nothing has happened," she told him. "Go and find out where this place is, or let one of the others go, but we can't just sit here waiting for something which might not happen."

He thought about that, knowing that she was right as she usually was but looking for a way to rationalise it to himself other than just being bored of waiting. The reason for stopping at the camp had been to recuperate, which they had been doing until someone had strolled up to their front door, but packing up everyone and leaving without an objective seemed too much like a step backwards. Leaning over to give her a kiss despite her squeals about the beard, he left to find the others.

Thirty minutes later, he was leaning over a large-scale map with Mitch and Leah.

"The ERV needs to be some distance away," he said, as though Mitch needed a lesson in the skill which had been second nature for most of his life. Realising that the explanation was more for Leah, he nodded along with Dan.

"ERV one, here," Dan said, pinpointing a large bridge to the south. "Wait until daybreak on Monday then fall back to ERV two."

That gave him a minimum of three days to catch up with them if they had cause to leave without him.

"ERV two, here," he said, this time indicating a small settlement at least thirty miles to the south; it was far enough to not be in the same area but not so far that it couldn't be reached on foot within the agreed forty-eight-hour time limit.

"After that, we look after ourselves," he finished lamely, breezing over the worst-case scenario.

He straightened up, his back cracking in the process, and looked at the wider picture of the map. He had three days allocated to finding a better radio signal: one to travel southwest inland on the straightest and hopefully fastest roads, one to climb up high and get more of the message, and a day to travel back. Should he find the camp deserted in case the others had reason to leave, then he would turn around and head south to meet them at the bridge. If that failed, then they would fall back again and if that then failed, he had no idea what would become of any of them.

The planning of emergency rendezvous points before the group split was commonplace, but never had they found themselves planning for so many people over such a huge scale. The discussions of failure brought more than the usual amount of trepidation on the eve of something big: it brought fear this time. Dan had thought through his options and requirements, deciding that he had to use something more substantial than the motorbikes they brought for scouting. He would need to take additional fuel, equipment and supplies if he was to be away for more than a night. That meant causing a huge stir in the camp by having to move the big truck out of the entrance and manoeuvre the most readily available of the smaller trucks they had.

Despite his disappointment, getting the armoured truck out would take too long and be too disruptive, so he reluctantly took the lightweight army Land Rover complete with its cracked windscreen where it had been perforated by bullets only hours after they had acquired it. He threw in his battered black rucksack, which had barely left his side in well over a year, as well as two jerrycans of diesel, a sleeping bag and a whole slab of bullets. He liked to be sure.

He was going alone: they all knew they couldn't face the loss of two guns while they were still on high alert, but the question remained of whether Ash should accompany him or not. Three days without the dog would cause them both a fair amount of anxiety, but the pros and cons of leaving him with Leah were discussed. His early warning system could prove invaluable should anyone else decide to pay them a visit, and while it would be beneficial to Dan, he knew that he was effective enough alone. As much as it tore at him, he took his dog for a walk and told him he would have to stay behind.

"It's not that I don't need you or want you," he told Ash as he stared back at him with no comprehension, "but you're needed more here. I'll be fine and it'll only be for a few days."

Getting no answer back, not that he expected one, he ground out his cigarette on the ground and walked back to the others, planning to leave at the following dawn.

DARK, DAMP AND DANGEROUS

Eight miles out to sea, over a hundred feet below it, and almost five hundred miles away from Dan's uncomfortable chat with his dog, four people sat quietly in their very slow-moving vehicle.

The stress inside the truck was palpable, as much as the dank and foul air deep underground was slowly choking them. Without the small army of engineers and technicians required to keep the tunnel operating at peak efficiency as it had for over twenty years, the upkeep of such an astounding feat of engineering had been sorely neglected. The power to the air recirculation systems died long ago, and as a result, the quality of the air at the deepest section of the tunnel was desperately poor. They had decided, as logically as they could, to drive through the tunnel section the wrecked inbound train had used, hoping that would negate the chances of meeting any obstruction along the way which would force them to reverse for miles until they once again found daylight and fresh air.

Obviously, the logic was sound insofar as when the crash first happened, but the risk of an obstacle which fell into place after was still on the cards. They all knew their reasoning was weak at best, but removing the chances of finding an outbound train completely blocking their route offered some small comfort.

Not that comfort was a concept they could fathom at that point; the air was literally thick and had a quality unlike anything any of them had ever experienced. It was more of a taste than a smell, but it was undoubtedly unpleasant. Even through the closed windows with the air inside the car set to recirculate, their supply of oxygen was being slowly eroded. It started with the occasional cough, but now after almost an hour underground, it was becoming more of a problem. At their current rate of travel, they would need nearly another hour to get clear on the other side.

In another hour, they would probably all be too hypoxic to operate a vehicle.

In another hour, they would probably all be well on the way to being dead.

RIDING SOLO

As he always did, Dan left with as little fuss as possible. Leah saw him off with Marie and Neil at her side. Dan held her tightly, worried that the woman carrying his child was still looking exhausted to the point of appearing almost grey in colour.

"What's your plan again?" Leah asked with professional curiosity.

"Drop about a hundred or so miles south–" he began.

"Kilometres," interrupted Leah, prompting a look of annoyance.

"I'll drop about two hundred kilometres south and after that I'll cut away for higher ground," he answered sarcastically.

Nodding her agreement at his plan, Leah still wore a look of confusion as she tried to formulate the equation between the metric and imperial measurement systems.

"One point six to one. Ks to miles," Neil offered, seeing her struggling with the mathematics.

Waving Dan off, Leah turned away to check her distance-string calculations on her map.

Driving away on his own, he felt suddenly so sure that he was being intensely watched, so much so that he actually began to scan the higher ground for any telltale sign of a watcher with an optic catching the rising sunlight.

He saw nothing and told himself that he was just being paranoid.

"Two minutes in the car on your own and you're already bloody talking to yourself!" He laughed, realising that the joke wasn't entirely inaccurate. Or funny.

Sacrificing caution for speed, he turned off towards the larger roads, slowing only to snap off the plastic barrier as he drove through a tollgate before accelerating as hard as the uncomfortable truck could manage. Eyes alert and scanning as far ahead as he could manage, he relished being free and moving again.

He often felt too contained before, but this was different. Getting away from home and ranging out even a day away took the edge off his uneasiness, but being totally nomadic was less enjoyable than he imagined. Perhaps, he thought, being unburdened with the responsibility for the others he would be happy just driving around with his dog and his guns.

But then again, he pondered, he might just be as wild and unpredictable as some of the worst people they had met without the tether of a group to ground him. To keep him sane.

Marie had told him once when they were talking about Rich overcoming the crippling post-traumatic stress disorder which left him so unable to integrate sometimes that his own situation was vastly different to most other people. Dan was broken before the world ended, and bizarrely the apocalypse fixed him, whereas it left most other people depressed and emotionally shattered.

He was socially awkward at best, he knew that. But in truth, and in spite of all the disturbing events he had experienced since he found himself alone one morning, he had a purpose and a reason to stay alive. His purpose now was to put in at least a hundred and fifty miles, or two hundred and forty kilometres for the sake of argument, before he cut away from the abandoned toll roads; further than he had originally decided.

Cruising along at a comfortably sedate fifty miles an hour, he guessed he was making as much progress as he could hope for. Any higher speed made such a skull-piercing noise from the all-terrain tyres that he found it impossible to concentrate on driving in a straight line. He passed only the occasional vehicle and avoided the small rest areas which were scattered intermittently every ten kilometres or so. Logic dictated that anyone suffering illness would stop their vehicles, and he knew – even if they didn't at the time – that they would never rejoin the road. He carried on, unwilling to view the sad scenes of people dead in their cars.

He cut away to the smaller roads after two hours, aiming the breezy truck towards a supermarket of such epic proportions that he couldn't imagine finding anything comparable back home. Approaching slowly, he slid from the driver's seat and stretched out his aching muscles. Restoring the ugly shotgun from the dash to the sheath on the back of his vest, he checked his weapons more out of obsessive compulsion over a technical need, and walked cautiously towards the large revolving glass doors. Giving an involuntary click of his fingers for Ash to fall in, he silently cursed himself for not remembering his shadow was left far behind with the others.

Forcing the unpowered door to grind around sufficiently to allow him in, he saw that the sealed portion was full of dead leaves, rotten away into mulch. Taking a second to understand what that meant, he realised that someone must have been here the last time the leaves had fallen from the trees.

Knowing that nobody had used this door for almost a year was both creepy and reassuring.

Taking a knee and listening intently, he heard no response to the small noises he had made getting inside. Still, he hadn't lived this long by being careless, he thought to himself. Creeping along aisle by aisle, he took note of where some bottles of water were for retrieval. The consumable food had rotted away long ago, leaving nothing but dried puddles and dirty marks where the insects had gorged themselves months ago. Finding the section he needed after passing large displays of refrigerators and garden furniture, he began to sift through the dust-covered books until he found what he wanted.

A French–English dictionary. One of only two on the shelves and right now worth its weight in gold to him. Not wanting to hang around in an exposed area without backup, he stuffed the dictionary into his vest and swung back via the water aisle to grab himself a plastic-wrapped brick of natural mineral water.

A quick scan outside showed no cause for concern, so he threw his small haul back into the truck and drove out. Surviving in an exposed environment, especially alone, was more luck than judgement sometimes and he felt lucky that nobody was there to take an interest in him.

Deciding to push another hour inland, he settled back into the seat and eased the speedometer back up to almost sixty as he tried to ignore the tyre noise.

Setting his sights on the far hills, he drove along, eyes still alert to any potential danger.

Three hours' drive behind him, Mitch stood watch. He had an uneasy feeling, unbeknown to him the exact same feeling Dan had as he drove away: he was absolutely sure he was being watched. Just as he convinced himself that he was imagining it, the sound of the single shot echoed around the valley.

At the exact same time, the bullet hit him straight in the chest, throwing him off the top of the truck and bringing the ground rushing up to his face with sickening force.

LIGHT AT THE END OF THE TUNNEL

It was more of a physical reaction than a conscious thought, some deeply ingrained survival instinct which took over and made his limbs operate the vehicle without the need for cognitive intervention.

Simon was drowsy. He could barely speak coherently, let alone realise that he was slowly suffocating and suffering the dangerous side effects of a loss of oxygen to his brain.

Simon's body, on the other hand, knew exactly what was going on. It couldn't articulate the fact that the fumes that deep in the tunnel were making the air almost unbreathable, or that the mix of gases there was toxic, but it knew that it was going to die if it stayed there.

It didn't weigh up options or consider possible outcomes: it just reacted. It made his right foot press down harder on the throttle and push the speed up to a bone-shaking and painful speed. His body was unaware of the fact that two of the other occupants were complaining loudly about this, even less aware that the third passenger was unconscious; it just forced them all towards clean air and sunlight before they suffered worse than the fumes they were currently breathing in.

Twice they bounced painfully over the rails and skimmed along the filthy concrete walls surrounding them as the headlights burned a bright white lance in front of them.

Imperceptibly, the air quality changed. The dimmest hint of grey infected the inky black around them and grew like an insidious virus, slowly taking over every minute part of their subterranean world until they began to realise they were approaching the other side.

Simon became more aware than he had been before. Not that he realised he was less aware at the time; it was more like the feeling of being drunk but not knowing why or how. He tightened his grip, squeezed the steering wheel and steeled his resolve to head directly for the light at the end of the ever so slight incline.

Like some hideous interpretation of birth, the Land Rover burst into the sunlight and skidded to a stop on the gravel of the tracks. Throwing open the doors, they spilled out to suck in as much fresh air as they could possibly inhale. Lexi was the first to regain her senses fully.

Dragging Chris from the car, she laid him on the ground and checked for signs of breathing which, with great relief, she found easily. Rolling him over onto his side with his head in her lap, she just sat and rocked as the others breathed through their own problems.

Trying to speak aloud, she choked and coughed uncontrollably. Clearing her throat, she tried again, this time in a strangely cracked voice which didn't sound like her own.

"Welcome to France," she said with heavy sarcasm.

PEACE IN SOLITUDE

Armed with his precious literature, Dan made good headway throughout the remainder of the day. Devoid of any recognisable sign of human life, the landscape he moved through became more undulating before the distant peaks became less distant. As the sun began to sink, he selected and cleared a small building to use as a shelter for the night. Finding a small slice of happiness in stretching his legs and only having his own wits and weapons to rely on, he made camp and ate a hot meal.

On further consideration, he felt that the happiness and freedom may have more to do with not having the others relying on him. A stab of guilt hit him, soon brushed under the metaphorical carpet of his thoughts, and he focused on the job at hand. Nestling into his sleeping bag for the night, he soon missed the company of one of the group. As the evening temperatures became distinctly more autumnal, he wistfully imagined the heat that Ash would be radiating right now.

As first light rose, so did Dan. The surprise at seeing his own breath misting in front of his face made him worry that autumn was further along than he feared, only for his mind to catch up and recognise that the drop in temperature was likely due to the significant rise in altitude. That elevated altitude was the sole reason he was there: higher ground and hopefully a stronger radio reception.

Fuelling himself for the day by cooking breakfast, he concentrated on the minute details of his routine. Open the plastic bag and ignore the written instructions, place the foil packet containing his favourite all-day vegetarian breakfast inside and pour in a distinctly unmeasured amount of water, seal bag and wait.

Inside of the anticipated thirty seconds, he watched as the bag suddenly inflated and steam hissed from the minute vents where the seal wasn't perfect. Knowing that the sachet of chemicals was now reacting with the water and creating a fearsome heat which, in turn, was being transferred to his breakfast, he sat back and glanced at his watch in order to count off the required eight minutes.

His patience broke just after six, and he ate the mostly hot contents straight from the silver packet, ensuring he scraped it clean with the folding spork he kept in his vest. Licking the last remnants of food from the utensil, he dried it on his trousers and returned it to its place. Not very hygienic, he thought to himself, but smiled that there was nobody around to admonish him for his lack of decorum.

Pushing the hot remnants of the rubbish aside from any potential prying eyes, he repacked his kit and stretched off in the chill morning air as he smoked. Taking the time to enjoy the nicotine now pumping around his body, he scanned the horizon for the best place to head for. A similar hill to last time with a radio mast already in place was the obvious choice, but he could see no easy way to reach the summit. He settled instead for the outside choice of a nearby tall building.

Population centres had been something he had actively avoided for months now. It seemed to attract the wrong kind of attention, like any survivor found there would hold no interest in growing food but instead would prefer a more piratical approach to gathering supplies. His confidence in having seen no sign of others for twenty-four hours led him to decide on the simple option of the nearby four-storey brick mausoleum.

As he approached at low revs, he killed the engine to roll in silently as he swung the front of the truck around so as to be pointing towards escape should he need to depart in haste. A slow circle of the building gave him no cause for concern and the discovery of an external metal staircase seemed just too easy.

Maybe his luck had changed, but he realised he had thought that before.

With a torturous noise, the rusted ladder squealed towards the ground when he pulled it. Fearing that the sound would have carried far, he took cover and watched to see if anyone was attracted to it. Nobody came. He climbed the ladder slowly, feeling that distinctly unpleasant sensation of vertigo as he looked down and could see through the steel mesh of the landings as he climbed.

Finally, with shaking hands, he found purchase on the rough shingle of the flat roof and hauled himself onto sturdy ground. Taking a moment to catch his breath, he then produced the radio from his pack and sat at the base of the building's aerial. He wound the device, lit a cigarette and meticulously laid out his notepad and pencil.

Ensuring the dial was resting at just after the 600 mark, he began to fine-tune it one tiny turn at a time.

Almost immediately, he was rewarded with a period of deliberate silence over the static before the familiar sound of the French voice repeating what he was sure was a recorded loop, only this time the signal was strong and the voice gave meaning through its tone rather than the words it spoke.

The tone of voice implied strength, compassion and safety.

Or perhaps he imagined it. It could mean danger, threat, superiority. He surprised himself with an uncharacteristic amount of hope and trust, and convinced himself that this place, wherever it was, could be somewhere they could be safe.

Checking over his previous notes, he wrote down the words he recognised again. He listened to the loop ten times over before he turned his attention to the dictionary.

Unaware of the passage of time as he concentrated on the pieces of the first puzzle requiring brains over all else since the world had turned upside down and inside out, he worked through all possible meanings of the message:

"Calling all survivors. We offer security, food and family. Our city has stood for generations. We are strong. We live and offer life. We are Sanctuary. Fort of the south sea."

Leaning back and saying it aloud, he repeated the message to himself over and over. With each repetition, he invested more passion, more meaning and more feeling than before until he finally believed in it. They now had a goal. A purpose. A destination.

Wherever it was.

Dragging the large-scale map of the country from his pack, he began to scour his finger along the coastline looking for any mention of a sea fort. His only memory of such was on the west coast and he recalled from some distant repressed past that a bay near Bordeaux was important during the Napoleonic wars which had raged over Europe. Shaking away the irrelevance, he continued down over Normandy, skirting the west coast of the map until he reached Spain. Skipping out the peninsular on the basis that the message wasn't in Portuguese or Spanish, he rejoined the coastline just after Barcelona.

And was rewarded with the words "Sud mer fort".

"South sea fort," Dan said to himself ponderously. "Sounds promising."

He checked and rechecked the entire French coastline on the map until no other option seemed possible given the information he had. To be thorough, he even dug out a larger-scale map to see if any of the French-controlled islands of the Indian Ocean made any mention of a fort, but he found nothing. Happy he had ruled out any other possibilities, he tried to calculate the distance he would have to travel to reach the promise of sanctuary.

Somewhere between six and eight hundred kilometres of unknown territory lay between his group and safety. Days if not weeks of travel if they encountered anything but good fortune.

The prospect of a continuing journey and a renewed race against time steeled his heart once more. It was time to go to work again and end the wistful daydreaming of camping in the woods and drifting around the empty countryside alone.

Only he wasn't alone, he realised. Voices from below were now distinctly audible over the looping message still playing on his wind-up radio.

The sudden drop in his stomach indicated the all-too-familiar payload of adrenaline surging through his body and preparing the muscles to fight as his senses sharpened. Instantly forgetting all senses which weren't immediately necessary, his heart rate rose and he could no longer feel the cold seeping into his body from inactivity.

Leaving the radio as it was instinctively so as not to alert anyone to a change in the environment's atmosphere, he crept towards the parapet and inched his head slowly over the ledge. Fifty feet below him were two people looking around his vehicle. Speaking in low tones to one another, they were obviously discussing the sudden arrival of an alien object into their world. As one of them reached the canvas back and lifted it to look inside, Dan's fear of losing his supplies and transport forced him into action.

Rising to one knee, he flicked the fire selector on his carbine and cleared his throat loudly.

The two explorers froze before wildly looking around for the source of the familiar but unexpected noise.

Happy with his height advantage and fearing no threat from the two unarmed men below, his only risk was damage to the vehicle if he had to fire. Preferring a diplomatic solution, he called out to them.

"Up here," he said, trying to invest his voice with enough force as to command respect but not inspire fear.

Fear made normal people do very abnormal things.

Keeping the weapon trained on them but not appearing to be actively aiming at a target, he stood and placed his left foot on the ledge. Being so close to the edge made him uneasy, but not as uneasy as not knowing the intentions of strangers.

As one, both men looked up as the movement caught their attention. As one, both men panicked and threw their arms in the air as both began to speak at two hundred miles an hour.

"Je nes comprends pas!" he shouted down in what he was certain was an awful pronunciation.

Both men stopped talking. One shouted back up in a similarly poor accent.

"English?" he asked.

"Oui. Anglais," Dan replied loudly, as though sheer volume could overcome incomprehension. "Don't move. Stay still, understand?" he shouted, reinforcing his words with a hand gesture as though he were instructing Ash to sit.

Abandoning the radio where it sat to maintain sight of the two at ground level, Dan sidestepped to the left until he found the ladder. Quickly slinging the weapon behind him, he dropped one level before bringing it back to bear on the vehicle.

Neither of the men had moved.

Repeating the process for each floor he descended made for slow progress, but eventually he was restored to ground level and approached them with legs bent and weapon raised. Stopping at twenty feet, he shouted at them to drop any weapons, resulting in confused looks being exchanged between them.

"Weapons," Dan shouted again, tapping at his own gun with his left hand. Finally, they seemed to understand, and a single semiautomatic pistol and a hunting knife were dropped to the ground. Moving in and kicking the weapons aside, he switched to the Walther which he drew from the holster on his vest while simultaneously lowering the carbine. Patting them down in turn, he found no further cause for concern and relaxed to stand upright and collect their weapons.

The gun was in a poor state and probably hadn't been cleaned since it was looted, probably from a police officer, given that it was a mass-produced variant of a popular weapon.

Up close, the two men were both young and distinctly non-threatening. Both were thin and dirty, more like street urchins than the intrepid explorer of the post-apocalyptic world as he must have seemed to them. Feeling suddenly ashamed of having frightened them, he stowed his weapons and produced his cigarettes to offer them both one. Exchanging looks of fear as though it were some kind of trick, they edged forward, unsure. After they had both taken one from the outstretched packet and not been struck down, they seemed to relax. Dan offered them his lighter to use at a safe distance and watched as both began to relax.

It became clear that neither spoke English any better than he spoke French, so an uncomfortable silence reigned over the three men.

Dan had what he had come for and saw no sense in extending his trip now that he had a goal to pursue. Reaching into the rear of the truck, he pulled out a sealed box of spare rations which he had brought just in case.

Dropping it on the ground, he made a gesture of offering it to the two hungry-looking men who still stood awkwardly as though they did not know if they were permitted to leave or not. Both stared at him dumbstruck as he climbed behind the wheel, started the engine and drove away.

Glancing in the wing mirror, he saw the two men ripping into the box before he was even out of sight.

"See," he said to nobody with a smile of satisfaction, "I don't shoot everyone."

SUDDEN DESCENT

The ringing in his ears from hitting his head on the ground was so intense that he heard nothing until the sounds of desperate gasps for breath cut through the whine. It took Mitch a half-dozen precious seconds to recognise that the gasping came from him. The force of the impact had been lessened by the vest and spread out more evenly across his upper body, but the deadly impetus of the bullet hitting him directly on the sternum drove all the air from his lungs and left him winded.

As his hearing began to return, so did his other senses; hearing screams and shouts of panic and seeing people running around all fought for brain space to be processed.

Pushing straight to the front of the line was the sensation of intense, debilitating pain. Forcing it away as best as he could, he tried to shout for everyone to take cover but could barely utter a sound. Shaking his head as though the physical action could clear the fog from his synapses, he tried to stand only to hit the floor again. Constructing a painless fortress inside his head, he took precious gulps of air into his spasming lungs and willed the world to stop spinning.

Leah was sitting in the main building with Marie when she heard the shot. Springing to her feet, she snatched up her rifle and headed for the door, ignoring the panicked questions from behind her just as the first shouts were heard. Pausing before she went into the open, she took cover and peered around the corner to try and ensure she wouldn't be cut down by whoever or whatever posed them a threat. Was it an attack? Was it an accident?

Unbidden, Ash fell into position at her side on full alert, having reacted to the urgency with which she moved. Seeing no immediate threat, she moved fast and low towards the sentry position for answers. Taking cover at the rear of the biggest truck, she checked around the corner to see Mitch was down and struggling to get up. Fearing the worst, she bawled his name and was rewarded with a weak flutter of a hand in response as he turned to look at her.

"Are you hit?" she yelled.

"Vest. Not gone through," he managed to answer in between gasps as he tapped feebly at his chest.

As it dawned on Leah that she was now the most able fighter there, she had to formulate a plan and fast. They had to evacuate, obviously, but without knowing where the threat was, they couldn't blindly run away, or they could face more danger than they already did. Pausing for a second, she shouted at the top of her voice: "Everybody on the truck. NOW. WE ARE LEAVING!"

Her terrified companions needed little encouragement. People emerged from doorways and ran holding their belongings to the back of the truck where they threw themselves in haphazardly. Neil emerged from where he had been sleeping and looked around at the chaos until she caught his eye and pointed towards the cab for him to get it started.

"Adam!" she yelled.

"Here," came the response from the other side of the truck before he jogged around to her.

"We need eyes on; Mitch is down and we don't know where the shot came from. Don't expose yourself." She added the last words as she grabbed the front of his vest to be certain he understood her. He nodded and ran back to the other side where he could climb onto the bonnet for a better look.

She ran to Mitch and knelt at his side to check him over. Looking back, she saw Marie being helped along, quite unnecessarily, by Kate, who was more trying to shield her from any potential harm than hold her upright. Marie slapped at Kate's hands and pointed to Leah kneeling by Mitch. Without a word, Kate abandoned Marie and sprinted towards them, having seen someone in greater need of her skills. Sera followed, laden with the bags of equipment they needed as the joint medical team. Knowing that Mitch was in better hands than hers, Leah returned her thoughts to the immediate threat. She looked up to see that Adam had retrieved the big rifle and was scanning through the scope ahead to find where the shot had come from.

Still the steady flow of refugees spilled from the low buildings, making their way onto the truck. Leah thought how the withdrawal would work; there wasn't enough time to get everything loaded and all vehicles manned, but she couldn't leave behind the armoured vehicle or the fuel truck. If push came to shove, she would have to prioritise with fuel, but she couldn't bear the disappointment of losing the Foxhound. She thought Dan would be upset about that, even angry with her, then mentally kicked herself for daydreaming while in such a dangerous situation. She heard her name shouted from the front and ran around to find Adam pointing ahead as he handed her the rifle. Settling herself on the bonnet and using the top of the wall to the side to rest the big gun, she followed his instructions.

"Rocky outcrop. Ten o'clock, up and right. You see them?" he asked.

She did. An unidentifiable person dressed all in dark green and covered with torn-up grass for camouflage was barely visible. The dead giveaway was that something on them was reflecting the light, and from the resulting flash seen from their position, the shooter may as well have lit a fire. Breathing slowly out and holding her breath a few times, just as Dan and Steve had taught her, she nestled herself down to take the shot.

Breathe in, breathe out, hold.

Breathe in, breathe out, hold.

Breathe in, breathe out, hold, and squeeze.

Just as the person looking straight back at her similarly framed in a scope did the same.

Taking up the trigger pressure carefully, Leah caressed the metal back towards herself gently so as not to snatch the shot. A millimetre difference at her end could mean a two-metre difference at the target end, and she wanted this bastard dead.

The huge noise from the gun made her flinch involuntarily, but she regained her composure in time to see the result. As the bullet left the end of the barrel at an impossibly high speed, it spun true towards its intended victim. Finding her enemy in the sights once more, she watched in satisfaction as the last few spurts of arterial blood from the ruined head fountained high into the air. Firing directly along the line of the body, Leah's bullet had taken them in the top of the head, cutting through the stone-hard skull not once but twice, then carried on through to sear a destructive path through the torso and on into the ground.

They were dead the split second the trigger was pulled, and Leah had no idea that a bullet had come her way at the same time. Her shot had been good, theirs hadn't.

Being afforded no time to congratulate herself on a fine shot, the sound of renewed screams and a curious war cry echoed from behind. Without thinking, she dragged herself upright and onwards to the roof of the cab, where she saw muzzle flashes and movement emerging from the treeline behind.

Dismayed, she realised that no sooner had they resolved the threat to their front did the true danger emerge to their rear. Still holding the big rifle and standing so horribly exposed, she raised it to seek a target only to find after precious wasted seconds that the distance was too short to be accurate with the distance scope. Resting it down, she swung her carbine round and began stitching the approach paths of these new attackers with short bursts of fire. Having quickly emptied her magazine, she threw the empty one into the pouch she kept free for such situations and slapped in a fresh one to continue the fire. Her reload had been slick and professional, but it was a talent born of sad necessity more than pride or fanaticism.

Unaware of her own efficiency, she emptied the second magazine and reloaded again just as she felt the first of the return fire disturb the air around her. Her ingrained sense of survival dictated that she should probably not be standing on the highest point totally skylined for everyone to aim at, so she rapidly dropped to ground level.

She heard the distinct sound of rounds fired through a suppressor and found Mitch had been loaded into the rear of the truck where, although looking very pale and pained, he began to methodically put rounds down at anyone foolish enough to show themselves in the open.

Realising she had completely forgotten that she was currently babysitting, she looked around wildly for her neglected dog to find that Sera had already ordered him into the truck, where he sat protectively in front of Marie, wearing a confused look.

Unable to count in the panic and disorder, she bawled into the truck to ask if everyone was there. Confused and terrified faces looked around at one another as the volume of fire intensified from behind. Along with the sharp bangs of small-calibre bullets came the louder booms of shotgun rounds and simultaneously came the tinny sound of lead rain as the shot scattered from the metal skin of the vehicles and made everyone instinctively duck down lower.

A roar of challenge sounded from the woods, as though some semblance of order had infected the momentum of the attackers, and as one, a line of men emerged from the trees at a run. The opening rounds from Mitch and Leah cut down almost a third of the invaders, but the impetus of the attack threatened to overwhelm them if they stayed as they were.

A hand tugging at her shoulder made her turn her eyes away from her targets for a brief moment to find Henry holding his hand out and demanding a weapon. Ignoring him and looking back to the front to select another victim, she stalked the head of a man which bobbed up and down from cover. Timing it perfectly, she fired a short burst just as he peeked out and dropped to the ground dead.

Again, Henry tapped her shoulder insistently, forcing her concentration away from the attack.

"No, Henry!" she snapped. "Get back!"

Having someone who had never fired a gun before choosing this precise moment to take part in his inaugural firefight was dangerous to say the least. Pushing thoughts of his stupidity aside, she tried to calculate how many were left to get safely on board before they could escape. Firing less carefully, just to increase the volume of fire in the hope of suppressing the attack, she concentrated on her job for the last few seconds it would take until they could get away safely.

Henry chose that exact moment to do the bravest and most stupid, ill-advised and reckless thing he could possibly do.

Having snatched a gun from the belt holster of Emma, who cowered with her precious laptop bag covering Marie, he jumped down and ran forwards, sending rounds pointlessly, wildly and inaccurately towards their assailants. Shouts of alarm and anger and fear followed his suicidal charge, but miraculously he remained untouched by the enemy's relentless fire. Almost believing himself invincible, he grinned widely as he fired until the magazine ran dry. His smile turned to a horrified look of abject fear to accompany the empty clicks coming from the gun, just as he looked left and right in terror for a way out of the situation he had placed himself in.

At that moment, Jack, the last of them to emerge into the ambush, turned away from the safety of the truck he was climbing aboard and ran to seize Henry's arm, dragging him towards cover.

Just as the bullets began to come in reply to the boy's charge did they make it to safety. Only at the last possible opportunity did two lucky bullets find their mark.

Letting out a bone-chilling howl of pain and shock, Jack dropped to his knees as the colour drained instantly from his face. Blood showed thick and fast at his left side as he slowly toppled forward to pitch face first into the ground.

As though in slow motion, Leah leapt down and ran to him. Dragging his arm over her shoulder and screaming in rage at Henry to help her, she took him to the truck where almost every available space at the back was filled with her friends pouring fire at the trees to give her time to restore them all to the incomplete safety of the truck. As Jack was hauled inside, with his last moments of concentration, he met Mitch's eye and reach a blood-soaked hand out to him.

Taking the offered item, the soldier's eyes widened at the small lump in his hand: a faded dull green cylinder with its rusted ring pull-on top. The yellow stencilling bore the faint marks SMOKE SCREEN-ING.

So many questions as to how and why Jack was in possession of such an ancient and destructive piece of hardware bounced around his mind. Shaking away the confusion, he pulled the pin and held the short metal tube away from his body in fear of an early explosion, as though a mere arm's length would save him.

"Tell them to drive. Now!" he screamed, and he waited until the message was relayed forward and the truck began to move before shouting back at those still trying to find space to fire at the emerging invaders who had taken the opportunity to press their advance. "*Everybody down!*" Mitch roared, then, ignoring the terrible pain in his whole body, he drew back his arm and threw the cylinder towards the attackers.

The incendiary grenade exploded, bursting bright white smoke as though a firework had ignited at ground level. The thick smoke gouted outwards, pouring white-hot fire throughout the edge of the trees and cremating everything it touched, including the men. As they drove away, abandoning their fuel stores as well as their other vehicle, the pain returned to him and he knew that he had failed them. Watching Kate and Sera work on Jack brought a tear to his eye, before he blessedly lapsed into unconsciousness.

Leah now had the sound of dying men being roasted alive to complement her already recurring nightmare of savage dogs ripping the flesh from her bones.

WITHOUT SO MUCH AS A GOODBYE

Dan's return journey was even more unremarkable than the outbound trip had been. Feeling better about almost everything, a strange sense of satisfaction and achievement washed over him as he drove steadily back to the group to tell them the news. If they could make it to the south coast, and if the people broadcasting the message were still there, it would make finding help to cross to Africa much easier.

If that worked, then they had a goal, an achievable undertaking, a quantifiable task.

People worked so much harder and felt happier about hardship if they knew what the end looked like, and in this case, it looked like somewhere safe. No more nomadic lifestyle, no more temporary reprieves from the permanent discomfort of daily travelling. After that, he had no idea what they would do, but he refused to allow his constant depressing pessimism to infect the elation he now felt.

Only stopping to rest once, to stretch out his creaking back made weak by too much time spent behind the wheel, he pushed hard to get back, eager to spread the news. He could almost picture Leah with her piece of string snaking along the colourful lines on the map to estimate the distance.

His reverie was shattered as their small haven came into sight at the far end of the valley he drove into. That sudden jolt of realisation hit him again, not fully understood or articulated but there all the same.

Something was amiss. Registering finally that the entrance to the camp was no longer blocked by the large truck and that smoke was rising lazily from the remnants of some form of fire, Dan's heart dropped through his chest and into the ground. The fear, anger, dismay and desperation he felt then threatened to consume him. He had been away from them for less than two full days – a matter of hours in the grand scheme of things – and he had returned full of excitement to find that their poor luck had struck again and it had struck hard.

He was the bearer of good news coming to lift the spirits of all of them, but instead he found evidence indicative of something so terribly wrong that guilt came in the second wave of emotional attack and forced a sob to escape from his mouth. Not caring if he was visible to the occupiers of their former temporary home, he stopped his vehicle to get out and lifted his carbine up to take in the closer view through the scope.

He counted at least twenty people, none of whom seemed to be on guard duty, and watched on in horror as they rifled through the supplies abandoned in camp. Curiously, fires still burned in places among the trees, and he wondered if his friends had been forced out by flame and the heavy white smoke which lingered menacingly.

The anger rose like a burning fury in him. Wanting nothing more than to stride straight through the gate and murder every last one of them to get answers, he knew he would die in any attempt alone. As he breathed deeply to ready himself for another long drive without any sense of elation, movement showed at the camp.

They had seen him.

They had seen him and the chase was on.

The grim irony was that he was being chased in his own vehicle, too.

As the armoured truck bounced recklessly along the pitted road towards him, his mind focused once more. Like a curtain of purposeful anger had descended over him, Dan felt the world slow down just a fraction as he perceived a simultaneous acceleration in himself. For a man who had experienced the intense sensation of a maximum dose of adrenaline so many times that he fully understood it, it was a rarity.

Dan could harness it: he knew what it did to him and he embraced the change. His responses and reactions were sharper, more precise and accurate. His senses heightened and his mind moved at such a speed that the information was processed and the appropriate response was beginning before he had even intended it.

Now, before the conscious choice of staying to fight or escaping became a consideration, he was already turning the key to fire up the engine.

Knowing the capabilities of both vehicles well, he knew that if he could stay ahead for just a few miles to the more open roads, then he could easily outpace the slower, far heavier pursuit. If.

Pushing hard, he looked in the wing mirrors and saw that the chase was abandoned long before it became unwinnable.

"Amateurs," he spat nastily as he watched the reflection of his own pride and joy shrink away into the distance, only to see one of his own motorcycles bearing down on him in the reflection. Incredulous at the sheer temerity of these attackers, he satisfied himself with taking at least one of them down and hurting them badly before he escaped. Weaving the Land Rover left and right as though he were trying to shake off the agile bike, he slowed slightly until he had hypnotised the rider into matching his pattern. On the next drifting movement left, he snatched the wheel back hard to the right and just as the startled rider tried to match the movement, Dan threw the wheel back to the left and stood hard on the brakes.

Catching the bike with his nearside between the wheels, he floored the accelerator again and was rewarded by the grinding noise of both rider and motorcycle passing under his rear tyre.

Gripping the wheel tightly as he kept the pace high, he steeled himself to create a big distance between him and these bastards.

It would take him another day to get to the rendezvous point, and he just hoped he wouldn't still be alone after that.

DESPERATE TIMES

Neil was behind the wheel of the big, unfamiliar truck as they bounced along the roads in flight. Overloaded with people and supplies, the engine screamed in pain as it was pushed to the very edge of its limits to make their freedom and safety a reality.

They weren't chased, nor was there an ambush waiting for them on the road. The sheer lack of professionalism in the attack made Neil's blood boil in fury: how could they have gained such a victory without the ability to plan even the most basic cut-off to ensure they captured them all? Unless they weren't after them. Unless they only wanted their shelter, or their vehicles or supplies.

Thinking of how many valuable resources they had abandoned made him wince. They had gone from having weeks' worth of food, thousands of spare rounds as well as backup weapons and parts to having little in reserve other than what they carried. They had lost all of their spare fuel, the thought of diesel making him glance down at the instruments in relief that he had topped off all of the fuel tanks when they were stationary. Further consideration of their fuel situation made him slow the truck down to extend their range; at the speed at which they made their escape, they would have suffered a breakdown or crash within the hour.

Hearing a thumping noise on the bulkhead behind him brought him back to reality. Adam and Jimmy were crammed in the cab beside him, and Sera's voice cut through to them.

"We need to stop. Jack's bleeding too badly," she yelled.

The risk of stopping so close to where they had been attacked was too great. Neil made the simple but brutal calculation: stop now and risk everyone's lives or continue and put Jack at risk of bleeding out.

The needs of the many.

When Steve had said that about them leaving, it had caused uproar. How can one person be so calculating, so callous, as to demean another person's life to a matter of mathematics? How can their conscience allow the words to escape their mouths, to accept their death without even trying to fight it just to claim responsibility for the unquantifiable survival of others?

As harsh as his thoughts were when the sentiment was uttered by someone else, he came to the conclusion quickly in his own mind.

"Tell them we have to keep going," he said in a low voice to Adam, who was sitting next to him as he kept his eyes resolutely on the road. "We'll stop as soon as it's safe."

Adam swallowed and stared at him, trying to phrase it as gently as he could before turning his face and calling back through the thin metal partition.

"We'll stop as soon as we can," he shouted lamely, offering no further explanation and receiving no answer.

Everyone had their priorities, thought Neil. To Kate and Sera, and he accepted most likely Jack, the priority was to stabilise him and stop the bleeding. The fact that a pack of armed hostiles may be hot on their heels driving their own stolen vehicles and firing their own looted bullets at them was an irrelevance to them at that moment. His priority was to put as much distance between them as possible, and he had to do that no matter what the fallout. Playing off longevity against immediate safety, he pushed the speed back up a little.

For another ten minutes, he heard nothing more. When the shouting and banging behind him raised in intensity, he could no longer ignore them and told Adam to say that they were stopping.

Pulling off the road, he made straight for a covered commercial garage with the roller shutters most of the way up. Not bothering with the time it would take to check if it was safe, he drove straight in nose first and killed the engine before spilling out to check for danger. A flurry of activity was happening behind him as he checked every corner of the large workshop they had so suddenly invaded, and seeing the manual overrides for the shutter doors, he slung his weapons and pulled hard on the stiff chains.

Calling for help, he was joined by other hands as they added their combined body weight to the task, eventually being rewarded with the screeching sound of seized metal giving way as the doors began to descend and plunge them into a murky, dusty darkness.

At the back of the truck, Kate was barking orders, as was her manner in an emergency. Having had a table cleared and dragged into a shaft of sunlight from a high window, she gave further orders as people brought her the things she needed. Seeing too many idle hands with the attached minds having time to panic, Neil gave his own orders and had the unit thoroughly searched and the exits secured.

While Kate and Sera were working hard on stopping the blood gushing from Jack's side, he found Leah still in the back of the truck with Mitch. She was gently easing open the stiff Velcro of his vest and lifting it away as carefully as she could so as not to cause him any more pain, just as Ash whined softly and licked at the dried blood on his face.

He was sleeping in a way; pain racked his body and forced his face into a rictus of agony as she worked, but blessedly he seemed oblivious to the worst of it. Pulling up his black polo shirt, she gasped at the livid bruising which had already radiated outwards from the centre of his chest. Suspecting that there may be a few cracked ribs too, she checked the rest of him as tenderly as she could, finding nothing else but a gash to his head, likely sustained as he fell, which had already stopped bleeding. Using the small straight-bladed knife she kept taped to the left shoulder of her vest, she dug the point into the vest she had taken off Mitch and began to work it around. After considerable effort, she retrieved a misshapen and ugly lump of lead where it had been stopped by the many layers of interwoven mesh. The vest had done its job and prevented penetration, but there was only so much that could be done, and the resulting mess of his chest was testimony to that. Any higher calibre and it wouldn't have been stopped by the layers, but without walking around bearing the extra poundage of the ceramic plates front and back, there was little hope of surviving such a hit. He was lucky.

Seeing Neil watching her, she suddenly felt embarrassed at having an audience but embraced it as she asked for help making him more comfortable. Clearing a flat space as she pocketed the twisted bullet remnant, she spread out a sleeping bag and together they gently laid him down with his head and legs raised slightly. Looking outside the truck, her eyes rested on the first unemployed pair of hands she saw and snapped at him for his attention.

"Henry!" she said, prompting him to jump in fright. "Get over here!" She waited impatiently as the older boy clambered up the tailgate to stand at her side.

"Watch him," she said nastily, pointing at Mitch. "If his breathing gets noisy or sounds laboured, then scream for help. Other than that, stay still and do nothing."

As she was about to turn away, she saw that Henry still had the gun tucked into his waistband and her temper snapped. Whipping back to him, she snatched the pistol away and rammed the muzzle hard up under his chin, forcing him back against the side of the truck. He squirmed his face away from the business end of the gun to no avail until Leah leaned in close to his face.

"Look at Jack," she snarled.

Henry's face didn't move, so she repeated the order while reinforcing it with a push of the gun. Henry turned his face to see people working desperately to help the old man.

"That's your fault," she whispered in his ear, before pulling the gun away roughly and jumping down. Ash followed with a glance at the boy before he flashed his teeth and followed suit by jumping down. Mortified, Henry looked to Neil for support or even to share in his outrage for being threatened and blamed, but he met no such agreement in his eyes. With a final look of disappointment, Neil too turned away and left the boy to his own conscience and duties.

Leah had rolled up her sleeves, stripped off her weapons and body armour, and threw in her lot to help the makeshift trauma team.

Jack was in a bad way.

Covered in blood, Kate worked with her hands on his left side to find the entrance and exit wounds. Eyes to the ceiling as she looked with her fingers, she called aloud the bad news. "Two entrance wounds at the back, only one exit front. We need to get the other bullet out," she said.

147

"What do you need?" Leah asked confidently.

Hearing the question, Kate turned to Sera and fired off a list of equipment she needed from her bags. It wasn't that she ignored Leah intentionally, but it was more that Sera understood her requirements more and there was precious little time for explanations. Unoffended, Leah carried on checking Jack over at the extremities, as she knew that their paramedic's priority was with gunshot wounds.

Loud swearing and screams of futile anguish came from the truck. Panicking that Mitch had succumbed to internal injuries that she could not have diagnosed, Leah's heart sank until she made sense of the words she heard.

Sera was beside herself with grief and rage as she reported the loss of Kate's equipment bag. "It must have been left behind in the panic," she shouted, tears pouring down her face.

Ever the practical mind, Leah asked Kate again what she needed.

"Sutures, fluid bags, IVs, dressings…" She listed these in a desperate voice without taking her hands away from keeping pressure on Jack's flank. "Everything," she said, finishing with such a sadness and air of futility that it threatened to overwhelm them all.

Leah was not one for futility. See a problem: find a solution.

"Neil," she said, catching his eye, "map?" Walking away from the makeshift operating table, she joined the older man in another patch of light as he spread out the map.

"A few hours to the ERV at least," Neil answered in anticipation of her question.

"And three days to make it there," she finished for him, "which we aren't going to do unless we get more medical supplies."

Neil was surprised at the different tracks of logic they seemed to be on. Perplexed, but fearing the answer, he asked outright. "What's on your mind, kid?"

"Somewhere close. Hospital, ambulance station, doctor's surgery. *Anything* that would have what we need."

Both scoured the map to find where they believed they were, settling in agreement on the outskirts of a large town. Fanning out from there, their fingers traced lines until the legend at the side of the map was consulted and what appeared to be a small hospital was located.

"It looks to be about three or four miles away," Neil said out loud as the thought came to him.

"Can't take a vehicle; attracts too much attention and leaves you all stranded," Leah responded in a similar distant tone as her brain worked overtime too.

"Hang on a minute," Neil said as the consequences of her words sunk in. "What do you mean 'leaves you all stranded'?"

"It means I'm going, now, and you're staying here," she told him defiantly, daring him to try and overrule her. Neil knew better than that; she was the better soldier, and she was younger and fitter with better reactions and sharper senses. But she was still a teenage girl, and it burned through his very soul to let her take a risk that he could take instead. Opening his mouth to raise all these points, he found himself cut down instantly.

"Don't give me any shit about someone going instead of me. I need to go, and you and Adam need to stay here to protect the rest and that's the end of it." With that, she whirled away, followed loyally by Ash, and began to replace her empty magazines with the full ones from Mitch's vest, as she didn't have the time to reload her own from the precious store of munitions in the truck.

Neil watched her as she checked every piece of equipment, scoffed down a cereal bar while barely tasting it, and followed it with a bottle of water. Fuelling the engine, that was all he had just seen her do. She didn't eat for enjoyment, only to ensure peak performance when needed. Seeing such a young girl be so robotic saddened him, but on balance he was happier that she was on their side.

"How are you going to carry it all back?" he asked her gently so as not to seem like he was trying to dissuade her.

Wordlessly, she climbed into the truck and looked at the wreckage of assorted bags thrown down. Finding the one she wanted, she opened the top and turned it upside down to scatter the belongings recklessly around until the bag was empty. Turning around, she threw the now empty bag to its owner and informed Henry that he was her packhorse.

Horrified, the boy just stood there with his mouth open watching her walk away until Neil told him that he was to go with her.

"Stay quiet, do exactly as you are told and nothing else," Neil said to the boy. "This is the only thing you can do to even begin to make it up to her."

Watching him go in a trance, Neil settled down to take over watch on Mitch's condition. Seeing the purple bruise of his chest gently rise and fall made Neil think that being asleep throughout all of this was an appealing option.

ARE WE NEARLY THERE YET?

Long journeys were a struggle for anyone. Being alone was bad, but sharing the experience with three others who really weren't getting along all that well made for significant discomfort. Even worse when the droning, repetitive whine of tyres on concrete left a monotonous ringing in her ears to complement the ache in her body brought on by the vibration of the road through suspension and wheels which were more designed for foot-deep mud than long stretches of pitted asphalt.

Three days of driving at this pace had led them almost to the centre of the country after finding the ruins of Paris in the distance to be a less than inviting sight. It took them the entire first day to get past the tangle of interconnecting fast roads where one obstacle had even been the total collapse of the motorway flyover, causing three roads to be impassable. The source of the collapse was evident in seeing the burned-out hulk of a full tanker embedded into the rubble of concrete support beam.

Sticking to the smaller roads was fraught with terror, as every movement seemed like an imminent ambush.

Now, a few hundred miles inland, they were settling in to the same dangerously boring routine taking the toll roads ever south with no real idea of where they would end up.

Sighing and tightening her grip on the wheel, she blinked away the sluggishness and focused on the empty road ahead once more.

Three feet away to her left and pretending to be fast asleep sat Simon. The crossing had scared him badly, and the feeling of being drugged and driving through a waking nightmare had shaken him to his core. He was a big man in need of space and craving the freedom he had enjoyed his whole life outdoors, so being underground was not an experience he wished to repeat any time soon.

His quiet moment of introspection was interrupted when he felt the vehicle slowing down. Not wanting to open his eyes to see what had caused the deceleration nagged at his conscience, but he favoured solitude in the balance of that moment.

His self-absorbed moment was then shattered when Lexi swore loudly.

"What the fuck?" she said with an element of terror in her voice.

Straightening in his seat instantly, Simon peered ahead and blinked his eyes into focus in search of what had caused her outburst. As she brought the car to a complete halt, he followed the line of her outstretched finger.

Squinting to make out what it was, the horrifying reality of a severed head impaled on a spike burned into his brain. Silence reigned in the cab for a few brief moments, before all four began to speak at once.

"Back!" Simon snapped at Lexi, who was already selecting reverse gear and half turning in her seat.

"Move your bloody heads!" she barked at Paul and Chris, who were obstructing her view as they both craned forward to stare at the gory scene ahead.

The tyres bit into the concrete and began to propel them backwards until she threw the wheel over in an arc to perform a wide turn.

Slamming the gear lever into first, she stood down hard on the accelerator again to speed away from whatever horrors waited down that road.

TIME-SENSITIVE

"It's got to be now," Leah answered angrily, making Marie take an involuntary step backwards and raise her hands to calm the girl. Neil had come to her in a last-ditch attempt to convince the girl not to go when he lacked the courage to try and insist.

While Marie was opposed to her going based purely on her age and the responsibility she felt for her, she couldn't argue that it made sense and her plan was fundamentally sound. Her only real concern was that she was insisting Henry go with her to carry any plunder she found. The untested and impetuous youth made Leah's task risky, but she couldn't find the words to get through to the girl. Her head swam, she felt dizzy, and knew that she would vomit uncontrollably very soon.

Guessing Marie's reservations, Leah preempted her in a bid to cut short the conversation.

"He'll do exactly as he's told and if he screws up, I'll bloody well leave him out there. Is that good enough for you?" she said icily.

Marie had to admit that those terms were acceptable. Before leaving to find somewhere private enough to give in to the sickness threatening to take over, she grabbed the girl in close and hugged her.

"Come back in one piece," she whispered before kissing her on the forehead.

Worried that the emotions bottled up that day would erupt if she were shown any more compassion, Leah pushed away gently with a promise that she would.

"Never make a promise you can't be sure to keep," Marie said sternly, echoing Dan's mantra. "Just be damned sure you look after yourself." With that, she turned away and walked as fast as her pride would allow to the small toilet in a back room.

Cuffing away an unauthorised drop of moisture at her right eye, Leah turned to see a very nervous Henry waiting for instruction. Raising a single finger to beckon him closer, she stared into his eyes to compound and reinforce the fear he felt of her. She needed him to be totally compliant and unthinking; the last time he had tried to be a hero had resulted in the carnage not thirty feet away from her.

"Stay close, keep your mouth shut, do exactly as I say and nothing else. Do you understand me?" she said in a cold voice, prompting only a demented nod from the boy, who was unsure whether his silence was required immediately or when they left the unit.

Hesitating, she reached down and hefted a pump-action shotgun. She held it for a moment and extended it to him. He reached for it, finding resistance in her arm as she held it tight. Glancing at her, he saw Leah's eyes burning intensely into his.

"Carry it for me and don't even think about trying to use it. It's Jack's, and he'll want it back." she snarled before letting it go and turning away.

She nodded to Neil as she walked towards the fire door adjacent to the large metal shutters. Emma ran up to her as she moved, thrusting a scrap of paper into her hands.

"Kate's written down the stuff she really needs. Good luck."

Leah nodded her thanks for both the list, which she had forgotten to ask for, and for Emma's kindness. The scientist wasn't one for sentiment and felt ever awkward around people and their feelings, so Leah was genuinely happy for the words she spoke.

Stacking up at the side of the door with Henry meekly following behind her, she whistled the dog once and watched with satisfaction as he loped towards her wearing his game face.

"He's my backup. You are just for fetch and carry. Got it?" She added one last snippet of advice to Henry. Turning back to Neil, she nodded once and pulled back the bolt on her rifle to load a round into the breech.

As the door cracked open to spill blinding sunlight into their gloomy hideaway, she stepped out fast to seek cover in case anyone was watching the building. Ash slunk low and fast with her, crouching down as she knelt behind a long-dead vehicle lying flat on flat tyres. Henry followed suit and Leah allowed herself a split second of cruel amusement seeing the sheer terror on his face. If he wanted to impress her, then today had not gone well for him so far, she thought.

Having studied the map as closely as she could, she turned left and began to move cautiously along the building line with Ash stalking at her heel. As instructed, Henry followed some distance back so as to still be close but not so near that he interfered with her drills.

The hospital only lay a few miles north from their position, but the whole journey there was fraught with risk, as every junction was overlooked by buildings bearing ominously dark windows. After thirty minutes of moving carefully, her legs burned from staying low and her breath rasped in her throat from the exertion. The same nerve-racking progress continued, and, to her surprise, Henry made only one mistake when he knocked over a metal bin and prompted a loud echo to reverberate around the deserted streets.

It took just over forty minutes before the hospital came into sight. It was a ruin to look at from the outside, with abandoned ambulances littering the main entrance. They didn't look like ambulances, but Dan had already educated her about the continental practice that most ambulances were more like taxis than the traditional and familiar big yellow buses she was used to.

Cowering ten paces behind her hiding spot, Henry became worried. She was just kneeling there, doing nothing for minutes as she just stared at the building. The supplies they needed were in there, so why didn't they just go and get them so they could run back to safety and be out of this unfamiliar and frightening world? But she didn't move, she just sat there watching and making him more and more nervous by the second. He was terrified. This was all he had wanted for the last year, everything he had hoped Dan would bestow on him: the prestige and status of being made a Ranger, the gun and the equipment and the training to go with it, but all of this he suddenly realised he didn't want. It was dangerous, and it scared him half insensible. Just as he thought he couldn't bear to stay still any longer and was considering running all the way back to the garage and to the tentative safety of the others, she moved.

Clicking her fingers to be followed, Leah glanced over and met his eye; the gesture wasn't meant for the dog's benefit but for his own. With a silent curse and much forbearance, he did as he was told and followed her as she made her low, slow approach to the building.

Slipping silently between the forsaken vehicles shadowed by the big dog, she became more aware of Henry's total inability to move quietly. Fighting down her urge to reprimand him again, she reminded herself that she needed the idiot to carry back all the heavy supplies they were there for.

As her boots crunched impossibly loudly on the detritus littering the floor of the entrance lobby, she felt herself relaxing: the place had no sense, no feel, no buzz of human presence at all. That could either be a good or a bad thing, as it depended on why there were no humans left around here who would have interest in medical supplies. Her mind drifted off to the abandoned supermarket and the foul pack of dogs who had claimed it as their territory.

Knowing that she would be able to search far more effectively as just girl and dog, she deposited Henry to hide behind the reception desk, giving strict instructions to do absolutely nothing under any circumstances. Creeping further into the decaying building, she tried door after door to search for a supply room.

Every minute she was away from Henry, she felt safer, as though the boy were a magnet for danger. Contrastingly, every second she was away from him made him feel more and more exposed, as though she represented safety and protection from the appalling sights of the world they inhabited.

As she checked one room, Leah tried not to look at the desiccated remains of the three people still in their beds. The one thing of interest, however, was the wheeled trolley which sat proud and dust-covered in the centre of the small ward. Looking around for the necessary keys, she decided that she had no stomach for searching dried corpses and elected to use the small crowbar tucked down the back of her vest just as Dan did when he cleared a building.

Splintering the wood easily, she saw a stack of tablets which would no doubt be useful. Wheeling the cart to the door, she left it in the corridor and continued her search. At each room where she located useful items, she repeated the process and placed them in the corridor for one single sweep to gather it all and be done. Glancing at her watch revealed that she had been searching for almost twenty minutes, and out of some small shred of compassion, she felt the need to check Henry hadn't run away out of fear or done some other kind of damage. Returning to the entrance lobby, she gave a small, low whistle for his attention and waited until the fearful eyes peeked over the counter which he had been hiding underneath. Twitching her head for him to follow, he made yet more noise as he tried to rejoin her side.

Holding a single finger to her lips just as he opened his mouth to speak silenced him instantly, not that they couldn't speak but more that she had little interest in hearing what he had to say right then. He followed her as instructed and began to load the selected items into the large rucksack as quietly as he could manage. She deposited him in a small office room as she extended her search and repeated the same pattern by returning for him to collect what she had selected. Pulling out the paper list from her pocket, she mentally ran through what she had already picked up.

"That'll have to do," she whispered to herself, prompting both boy and dog to snap their heads up to her as she spoke. Shaking her head at both of them, she arranged her equipment and led the way for the return journey, praying that they had got everything Kate needed to save Jack's life.

BROKEN THINGS

Dan had driven at the very limits of the vehicle for the last hour since he had crushed the foolish motorcyclist. Bizarrely, he was more annoyed at the loss of the bike than for the life he had taken; the person was nothing to him, just another unfriendly other who had foolishly crossed him, but the fact that he was on Dan's motorcycle stung him deeply.

He accepted that it probably wasn't the loss of the vehicles that hurt him most, but that his family was in the wind and only God knew if he would ever see them again. Still gripping the wheel tightly with his face set in a mask of pure hatred and fear, he drove on, desperate to make the rendezvous point and find them all smiling waiting for him. He chuckled to himself at the mental picture of them greeting him and laughing at his expense for him thinking the worst.

Realising that he was careering fast along the road with no concentration on the immediate frightened him back to the present with a jolt. Slowing down and checking the mirrors for the millionth time in the last hour, he shook himself out of the torpor he had settled into. He should make the emergency rendezvous point by nightfall; from there, he could only guess at the next step, so he concentrated solely on getting there.

Ditching the faster main roads at the next available exit, he once again drove through the tollbooth barrier and snapped it away with a small surge of satisfaction for his anti-establishment attitude despite the total absence of any authority who could punish him for his meagre crime.

Try as he might, he could not stop his desperation and paranoia insidiously creeping into the forefront of his thoughts. Stifling a sob of terror and loss, he stopped the car suddenly and skidded to a stop on loose gravel at the side of the road. Killing the engine, he took a dozen deep breaths and forced himself to stay calm.

Failing utterly, he scrabbled clear of the cab and nearly lost his footing on the soft ground. Drawing in one great lungful as he dropped to his knees, he threw his head back and roared a scream of pure anxiety that tore the air and echoed back to him long after he had finished. Dropping his head, he stayed slumped where he was, like some lethal pressure had been vented before it destroyed the machine from within. Still collapsed where he landed, he remained in place, the only signs of life being the occasional sob as he cried in silence to pour out the last of the useless fear and panic at losing everyone he knew.

He would never have let any of them see him like this. Only Neil had even come close to viewing Dan go into meltdown, and that was at the very beginning when none of them knew what they were going to do. The child inside him longed for the comfort of his loved ones, for his fluffy big pet dog, for his friends.

Only they weren't going to magically appear to him.

Only his actions now could dictate the terms of him being reunited with them and, he chided himself acidly, that would never happen if he carried on having a tantrum like a toddler at the side of the road crying to himself.

Get up.

Get behind the wheel.

Man up and do something about it.

His inner voice bullied him into action, forcing him off his knees and making him dry his tears and wipe the pointless shame from his face. Crying about it achieved nothing, he told himself. Only action would have any effect on his situation.

Putting back on his mask of being able to cope with even the slightest change of plan without regressing to acting like a violent child, he stood tall and climbed back into the Land Rover.

"You're still breathing," he said to himself in a low voice. Unhappy with how weak he sounded, he cleared his throat and tried again.

"You're still breathing. You're alive," he said again with more anger and passion. "You're alive and so are they."

Slamming a hand onto the wheel in petulant anger, he turned the key and drove away hard, determined to make the ERV point before they did.

CHANGE IN PERSONNEL

Steve woke in the morning, sweating as he usually did, to find himself alone. Jan was usually one of those people who slept for about three hours and seemed no worse for wear, so finding him absent was a concern.

He was utterly fundamental to Steve's plans, and someone he not only needed but wanted with him. From hearing how he spoke about his interactions with the others, it was clear to Steve that his lazy charisma made him popular at mealtimes and, although Jan told him that conversations were listened to and frowned upon by the guards, people crowded to sit near him. Knowing what Jan planned to do, coupled with his conspicuous absence, made Steve very nervous indeed.

Struggling upright and limping heavily to the sink in his room, he poured himself cold water from a jug and washed away the sweat from the night's uncomfortable sleep. He was in pain, which was a further concern for Jan's non-attendance, as he always brought Steve's morning dose of painkillers. Washed and wearing fresh clothes, he sat on the bed and waited.

And waited.

Just as his patience was about to break and he planned some rouse to call in the guard inevitably posted outside his door, the door opened and in walked a young female. The flash of recognition threatened to burst out of his mouth until the warning look she gave silenced him instantly. Playing the invalid again, he leaned back on the bed and moaned softly just as the guard followed her in. He stood just slightly too close and clearly made her uncomfortable, but she resolutely ignored his leering presence and tended to Steve with a feigned lack of compassion. Handing him two tablets and a cup of water from the small tray she carried, she watched on as he took them without making eye contact so as not to give anything away.

Placing the tray down, Alice made a point of taking her time checking his pulse and blood pressure while he stayed still with a thermometer under his tongue. Scribbling notes on a piece of paper as she worked, she glanced up at the guard whose eyes never left her face other than to wander to other parts of her body when she wasn't looking.

Seeing how he looked at her made Steve feel simultaneously angry and sick, but he was certain that the young girl had a better handle on the situation than he did. He wasn't quite sure what his part in the charade was just yet, but he resolved his nerve to wait and see how it played out. He remembered how he had been told that the girl – well, the young woman he admitted to himself now – had joined Dan's group just before he did under violent circumstances. He wondered if her father was here too, still bearing the horrendous scars as witness to the brutality of others.

Desperate to ask for news, to talk to her and seek some comfort in familiarity, he had to force himself to remain oblivious to her presence. After she had prevaricated as long as possible with the short medical process, she turned abruptly, knocking the small tray she had brought with her to the floor at the feet of the guard.

Through instinctive reaction, the guard immediately bent to pick it up as she had hoped he would. In that second of opportunity when his eyes were not on her, she snatched something from her pocket and shoved her hand into the small cavity between the mattress and Steve's lower back. As fast as a striking snake, her hand was back at her side just as the guard straightened wearing a sycophantic smile, as though the small gesture of chivalry would impress her in spite of his constant ogling.

Smiling back at him and nodding a shy thanks, she walked from the room with her head down and, Steve suspected, an intentionally suggestive snap of her hips as she left the room. The guard's eyes had not left her backside the whole time she moved, and the sickening smirk adorning his face made Steve bite down his anger as the armed man turned his gaze back to him. The smirk became a sneer, and just as abruptly as he was disturbed, he was once again alone.

Waiting thirty seconds, breathing steadily and listening to the sounds of muttered conversation outside the door until it faded into relative silence, he allowed himself to reach under his back and pull out the small scrap of paper.

With a shaking hand and squinting eyes, he looked at the thin paper bearing the blotted ink, waiting for the words to wash into focus and provide meaning. Written in obvious haste, he read slowly:

Steve, we didn't know you were still alive until recently. Most of us are still here but some people have gone missing. We're guarded everywhere we go and get split up if we talk too much. We've been put into jobs. I'm still in the hospital wing, but anyone who won't work gets taken away. We don't see them again.

We were so happy when we found out you were still here.
Lizzie was really worried about you especially. I don't know what
to do, but we can't live like this. Get better and help us. Please.

A

Realising that the message was written on poor-quality toilet roll, he read it over three more times until he was sure of everything she had said. Getting up from the bed with some difficulty, he went to his wash bowl and carefully disintegrated the message until it could offer no evidence to be used against Alice or himself.

With his head awash with facts, some newly learned and most simply confirmed, he tried to walk carefully around the room as he tried to figure out what the immediate future might hold. Where was Jan? Had they figured out that he planned to help overthrow Richards? Why had Alice been sent? Was it just a replacement for an innocent bout of illness or was it part of some game they were playing with him? Would the door burst open at any point with armed men coming to bundle him out for summary execution as a traitor? Was Jan already in a cell somewhere awaiting his fate?

The swirling possibilities made his mind spin so much that it hurt his head. Guzzling down some water to try and abate the pain building behind his eyes, he turned as the door opened once again without warning.

Frozen in fear that this was to be his arrest, his look of relief must have seemed laughable to the young guard who presented him with a plate of food. Nodding his thanks as he limped heavily over to the chair, he ate hungrily as he realised for the first time that he had not eaten that morning and it was already after midday. Without Jan, it

166

was obvious that he would not be going anywhere, so he instead resolved to work on his health for lack of anything better to do.

Getting slowly to the floor, he began to try press-ups but found that he could only manage a few before collapsing under the drastically reduced weight of his upper body. He tried to repeat the exercise with his knees on the floor, but stabs of white-hot pain seared down his damaged leg; he persisted as far as he could before lying flat on the floor to catch his breath. Turning onto his back, he tried to do some crunches only to find the similar sensation of being weak as a kitten. As he lay on his back panting, the door once again burst open and the guard stopped in his tracks to see Steve flat on the floor and clearly struggling.

As he stood and looked down at him, Steve conjured up the lie immediately to give an easy understanding to what the guard saw.

"I fell," he said in between gasps of breath, adding fictional pain to his false claim before seeing, with great relief, that his pretence had been accepted. Grudgingly, the younger man slung the rifle on his back and walked over to drag Steve upright with as little compassion as he could muster. Without another word, he left him sitting on the edge of the bed and walked away, returning with another plate of food and a small paper cup with two tablets in. That would be his nightly drugs then, he thought sadly, annoyed that Jan's unexplained absence had meant a drastic reduction in care and medication.

Eating the food and drinking a large cup of water to wash down the tablets, he lay on his bed and wished that someone had left something to read. As he lay awake for most of the night listening to the muted sounds of the outside world, he waited for whatever ill fate was bound to land squarely on his shoulders.

ALL FOR NOUGHT

Shortly after Leah had left, Mitch regained his consciousness and immediately regretted it. It felt as though there was a concrete slab resting on his chest, and every breath brought a fresh wave of nauseating agony. Each expansion and contraction of his ribcage lanced molten misery to every extremity and brought a forgivable sob from his mouth. Neil stirred at his side and leaned over to look in his eyes.

Mitch opened and closed his mouth before the smallest of coughs closed his eyes in torment. Seeing him struggle for words and eager to reduce the pain he felt, Neil told him what he thought he wanted to know.

"We got away after you threw that grenade. Jack's hurt bad and they're trying to save him now, but half of the medical supplies were left behind. Leah's gone for more," he said softly, stopping to hold up a placatory hand when the soldier's eyes widened to hear that Leah was outside alone.

"She's got Ash and she's taken Henry to carry for her," he said, cutting off any attempts at an interruption.

"Wasn't a grenade," Mitch whispered, sucking in a gasp of air as the pain in his chest renewed in the absence of adrenaline.

Neil couldn't hear the words he used so leaned in closer for him to try again.

"It wasn't a grenade," Mitch said through gritted teeth, sure to enunciate every word carefully. "White phosphorus. Old one."

Neil sat upright and frowned in thought; he hadn't seen one since early in his own military career. White phosphorus burned with a devastating intensity unless totally starved of oxygen, and he could only imagine the terror of the attackers as they roasted in the chemical fire. His mind wandered back many years to his own training, being told that they should never use white phosphorus to clear trenches because it was illegal, but that they would be really effective if someone accidentally dropped one on the enemy.

"Where did you get one of those?" Neil asked, shaking himself from the grim reverie.

"Didn't. Jack's," Mitch answered before coughing again and screwing his face tight with the fresh tsunami of suffering. His hand fluttered at the leg pocket of his trousers, prompting Neil to open it to help him.

On the subject of things people shouldn't have, he found a small single-use syrette of morphine.

Torn between wanting to reduce the suffering his friend was experiencing and feeling the fear of the unknown as he held the narcotic in the palm of his hand, he wondered whether he should take it away from him. Mitch still possessed enough of his faculties to snatch it from him and, before he could protest, removed the cap and jabbed the short needle into his thigh and squeezed.

With a sigh, his eyes closed and his breathing became steadier and no longer sounded ragged. A serene bliss overcame Mitch as he drifted into painless unconsciousness. Neil reached over and gently removed the used analgesic from his leg, carefully restoring the plastic cap over the needle and climbing down from the bed of the truck stiffly.

Glancing over at where the desperate fight for Jack's life was playing out, he noticed a distinct flurry of activity which made his heart sink.

Pip watched on in tearful horror as Marie told Kate she had lost Jack's pulse. She reinforced the statement by making sure Kate understood that the loss wasn't her fault; it was no longer there.

"Defibrillator," Kate called aloud to nobody in particular as she pushed people aside to begin chest compressions. Sera moved in to keep pressure on the bullet wounds as Kate nodded for her to step in.

"Defibrillator!" she snapped again, angry that nobody had fetched it yet.

"It got left behind," Sera told her after taking a breath to prepare for the onslaught she expected in return. Kate gave the briefest of pauses before resuming the chest compressions, but with every artificial pump of the heart, she forced a weaker and lesser amount of blood from the three ragged holes at the old man's side. No matter how much pressure she kept on the area, she could not hope to prevent the precious red liquid escaping.

"Kate," Sera said softly, and she was resolutely ignored. "Kate," she tried again, louder this time.

"Get another IV bag!" Kate screamed at nobody in particular as she carried on pumping the pale and lifeless chest.

"There aren't any," Emma answered timidly from behind her.

"Kate, he's gone," tried Marie, resting a gentle hand on her blood-covered arms.

"NO!" she said angrily with tears in her eyes. "We keep him going until Leah gets back with more fluids." With that, she pushed Marie aside and gave two breaths into his mouth to inflate his lungs.

Watching as the air hissed lifelessly from his throat, Kate resumed compressions. Sera took her hands away from the wounds and watched as barely a trickle of blood ran out with each pump. One by one, they inched away and left Kate still giving pointless CPR to their friend. The floor around where she worked was slick with blood. They were all covered in so much red that Sera realised there was little wonder nothing was coming from his body any more.

It was already out.

The people watching from the fringes of the area started to melt further into the shadows, unsure how they could help as Kate's actions went from an attempt at life-saving to beating a dead body with growing intensity.

Kate sobbed aloud now and repeated "no" to herself over and over. Finally, when she shifted her footing to gain better purchase to continue the chest compressions, her foot slipped in the great puddle of blood and took away her balance. Falling heavily to the floor, she tried once to get up but slipped again, landing further down where she lay her head down and cried aloud. Slowly, others moved back in to comfort her, until a blood-covered pile of women sobbed together as one on the wet ground.

Climbing down from the bed of the truck, Neil looked on in horror as he saw Jack's grey, lifeless body lying untouched on the table and those who had tried so hard to save him sitting on the floor in tears. An involuntary sob escaped his own mouth as the realisation of another death hit him in the gut like a train. Walking over to the table in a trance, he heard Kate's shocked statement above the crying.

"I could've saved him," she repeated over and over to herself.

Frozen to the spot for minutes, Neil just stared at the scene in front of him. Just as he wondered what he should say and do, a loud knock on the metal door snapped him out of his hypnotic state.

FINAL WORDS

Returning at a faster pace than their careful progress towards the hospital saw both Leah and Henry breathing hard while Ash stayed at her side with effortless physical ability.

Leah moved as fast as her standards would allow while still maintaining sufficient cover of the most exposed areas, but even so, she felt reckless. Henry was struggling under the weight of the heavily laden rucksack stuffed with the supplies they needed to replace what was lost in their escape. The supplies Kate needed immediately to save Jack's life.

Rounding the last corner before their temporary refuge came into sight, Leah checked the angles covering their path as best as she could, but found the same story as before: too many windows of taller buildings overlooking them offered safety to anyone watching them and posed a threat to them. Making the executive decision, she opted for the "fuck it" approach and ran for the door they had left less than two hours previously. Reaching it, she banged hard on the metal twice for it to be opened from the inside. Just as Henry caught up with her, the door creaked open and they spilled through and into the gloom from the failing light outside.

Snatching the bag from Henry, she ran towards the shaft of light bearing down on the worktop being used as a surgical bed and stopped.

Frozen to the spot with her mouth wide, she took in the abattoir scene before her.

Henry piled in behind and almost careered into her. Following her gaze, he froze as his worst fears were realised.

Jack was dead, Leah had failed to bring back the much-needed supplies in time, and it was Henry's fault.

Walking forwards as though in a trance, she dropped her rifle to the floor. With each zombie-like pace, she shed another piece of her heavy equipment, stopping only to lift the heavy vest from her slim shoulders until she stood in the glistening puddle of oily blood by the table Jack was lying on. Reaching out a tentative hand to touch his chest before pulling it away sharply, she turned and fixed her eyes on Henry.

Sensing he was now the target of not only the malevolent gazes of everyone present but also of Leah's fury, he turned to flee. Quite what he intended to do when he burst through the door into the harsh outside world he did not know, but he was prevented from ever finding out by Neil, who blocked the door; not out of any sense of helping Leah, but to prevent one of them from running scared into the unknown.

He turned in terror to seek another refuge, finding only that Leah had reached him in a few easy strides. Holding his hands up in front of his face and babbling incoherently, he felt the wind driven out of his chest by Leah as she brought her knee brutally up into his abdomen. Grabbing him roughly by the collar as he doubled over in pain gasping for air, she half-dragged him to the table where Jack's body lay. Sobs of fear, pain and guilt tore from his mouth as he tried pathetically to fight against his impending contact with the pool of blood. Leah was forced to switch her hold on him and bend his wrist painfully behind his back as she drove him forwards with the threat of a dislocated elbow.

Stopping before the table, she dragged him up to force him to look at the lifeless body of the man who had died for his stupidity, and then she let him go abruptly.

As he dropped to his knees and nursed the pain in his wrist, he heard the words she said to him: "You did this."

And then she was gone, and he was alone in front of a dead man.

"We rest until first light, bury Jack, then get to the ERV to find Dan," he heard Leah announce loudly to the group. He stayed where he was, the cooling blood soaking through his trousers and tainting his skin at the knees. He stayed there and cried out his shame and his guilt until his eyes ran dry.

Sitting around in whatever comfort they could find, the group ate and talked softly among themselves. Jack had been carefully cocooned in his sleeping bag and the sea of blood around the table was beginning to dry. Footprints led in every direction from the table, making cleaning the floor an impossible and irrelevant task. Henry sat alone in a dark corner of the dusty building.

Mitch had regained consciousness and was given far more mainstream painkillers than he had administered to himself earlier, although the pain was evident on his face with every breath. Marie broke the silence.

"I promised never to divulge any information that anyone ever told me in confidence," she said, hesitating over her next words, "but I think I need to share some of Jack's story with you."

Heads perked up at the prospect of learning a person's secrets; no matter what the terrible circumstances, human nature dictated a love of gossip.

"He was from the outskirts of Belfast, and where he grew up saw regular clashes with the Army. He told me about bombings, shootings, violence among members of the community over their allegiances, and how he was put to work as a young boy to act as a lookout. He progressed from there to become part of an organisation and," she hesitated again before continuing, "and he told me of some of the things he did as a young man."

Of all the people present, Mitch's eyes burned into her the most. He had served in Northern Ireland, had lost friends there and had his own life endangered many times by the political and terrorist groups who thrived in the underground societies to fight against the occupation of their country by British troops.

"He was not proud of the things he had done, more that he was caught up in a guerrilla war that was being forced onto the younger generations. My guess is that was how he came to have that grenade," she said, turning her eyes to meet Mitch's before continuing. "He left his home after seeing his brother killed and vowed never to go back to that life, so he moved to England." She smiled to herself as she looked down, one unconscious hand rubbing her belly. "He called it 'The land of my enemy', but he lived the rest of his life in peace. I'm sure

176

he would have put himself at risk for any one of us, and I hope that his sacrifice gives him the peace he wanted."

Silence hung over them. The revelation that their own Jack had been a terrorist in his youth was a shock to some, a painful and cruel joke to others, but on the whole, it made no difference. He was dead, and he died saving one of their own.

Hauling herself to her feet, Leah put an end to the reverie.

"We move in a few hours. Get some rest if you can." With that, she climbed into the truck and found somewhere to lay her head.

THE FEAR OF LONELINESS

Dan pushed on hard, ignoring potential risks in his heightened state of anxiety. He reckoned he could easily make the rendezvous point well before dark and played the scene where he was reunited with the others over and over in his head. Hours before, he had sped past the exit where a sign indicated a nearby hospital, oblivious to the terrible things being played out only a few miles away.

In his desperation, he had twice reached for the radio to try and raise the others, but both times logic took over and stayed his hand; if the group who had attacked them knew they were still in the area, it could end badly for them all.

It was a last-ditch card to play, but he convinced himself he wouldn't need to use it as he assured himself they would be waiting for him and they would all have a good-natured laugh at his red-faced panic.

Staying as positive as he could as he drove almost blind with the fear of being alone, he began to consider the worst-case scenario.

He would have to follow the plan if they didn't arrive by the third dawn and move to the second rendezvous point, but after that, he couldn't bear the thought of abandoning them. He would insist that they gave up all hope for him if the roles were reversed, but should they fail to arrive, it would become his life's mission to find them. Recognising that this course of action would likely reduce his life expectancy considerably made no difference to him; without them, he had no life.

Arriving at the marvellous expanse of the suspension bridge they had chosen to be the first emergency meeting point, he couldn't help but stare in wonder at the size of the great feat of engineering. Seeing something on a map gave no impression of just how big it was in real life.

It was empty, completely devoid of life, which meant that the best-case scenario was now off the table.

Carefully driving the length of the bridge to ensure it was still intact, he found it to be free of any obstruction and remarkably untouched by the brief passage of time without human attention. Turning around in a lazy circle at the far end, he pointed the Land Rover back towards the direction his friends should be coming from.

"Any minute now," he said to himself as he rolled the car to a gentle stop.

A few minutes later, he killed the engine to conserve his remaining fuel.

After two hours, his complaining stomach reminded him to undertake some personal admin: not that he felt hungry – his stress levels were too high to consider enjoying food – but more that his own tank was running too close to empty to make him efficient. Not bothering to go through the process of using the bags and water to heat the food, he ripped the top from a foil packet and ate the contents cold. He took no enjoyment from the slimy contents, merely used the process as a means to kill time.

His cramped muscles eventually forced him from behind the wheel and made him take a walk to ease his tense body. Opening the cigarette packet, he reached inside, feeling with his fingers to find nothing. Screwing the packet into a ball, he tossed it over the side of the bridge to see it snatched away by the wind. When he got back to the Land Rover, he rummaged inside his kit bag to find a replacement as he had done so many times before. His frustration and nervousness rose to a frightening crescendo as he found none. Tipping the whole bag out and scattering the contents, he sifted through desperately until he found his last packet.

Clutching it to his chest as though the life-shortening habit could sustain him, he ripped open the cellophane packaging like the addict he was and only relaxed when the first lungful of harsh chemicals burned into him. Closing his eyes and raising his face to the sky, he blew out a long stream of smoke, letting the worry disperse and a small sense of serenity return.

As the sun dipped below the far hill, he told himself that the others were being sensible; they would have hunkered down for the night in safety. Forcing himself to do the same, he climbed into the back of the truck and carefully repacked his equipment into his bag. Using the last of the daylight, he stripped and cleaned his weapons, taking such meticulous care that he had to rig up a light to finish the job. His concentration over the minute tasks helped him cope with the situation, and as all three guns were cleaned and oiled to keep them at peak performance, he glanced at the outside world to find it had grown dark.

With nothing else to do, he lay down his sleeping mat, unrolled his sleeping bag and nestled himself in relative comfort with his head on his pack. Keeping his boots on, he loosened his vest on one side as his only concession to comfort in the field. Being this exposed was something he would never do in his right mind, but the situation had driven him so close to despair that a part of him no longer cared for his own safety. Despite the agony of the loss he was starting to feel, he eventually drifted off into exhausted sleep.

Gasping awake after what felt like mere moments, he struggled to grasp the harsh reality of his situation. Calming his breathing and rubbing his eyes as though he could change the unwelcome truth by desperate will, he sucked in a sharp breath and held it. Letting it out slowly, he steeled himself for a stressful day of waiting and worrying. Climbing out of the chilly vehicle, he was surprised to see his breath misting slightly in front of his face. Trying to convince himself that a combination of the altitude and his exposed position was responsible for the lowering of the temperature, he couldn't deny the fact that autumn was in full swing and soon they would have to contend with savage weather conditions.

"He" would, not "they", he corrected himself depressingly.

Using the scope, he checked a full circle of his position to find, not to his surprise but to his dismay, that nothing had changed. Forcing himself to undertake the mundane and routine tasks, he set water to boil in the small shelter of one of the wheels of the Land Rover. Pulling open a ration pack again, he threw the first foil packet he laid his hands on into the water and checked his watch to give an indication of the required cooking time.

Bracing the cold weather, he stripped off to change his under-wear and T-shirt before dressing again and fixing all his equipment snugly into place. Using a mouthful of water from a plastic bottle, he brushed his teeth and spat a long stream of minty liquid over the side of the bridge to see it atomised and scattered by the wind.

Checking his watch to see that only a few minutes had passed, he draped an extra layer over his shoulders against the cold breeze and sat on the bonnet of the vehicle to smoke away the remainder of the cooking time. Dragging out every process to kill as much time as possible and maintain his sanity with every passing minute, he poured the hot water into a tin mug with a sachet of instant coffee and opened the foil packet of breakfast to let the steam vent. Returning to his perch, he resolutely watched the far end of the bridge as he ate lukewarm meatballs and pasta and drank tepid coffee.

If he was even close to being in his right mind, he would condemn his actions as foolish; to be so exposed without escape routes went against everything he knew. He was reckless, but he was alone and it clouded his judgement in worry. Sitting on the bonnet of his Land Rover, he stared at the approach, willing his friends to come.

And there he stayed, eyes fixed on the horizon, with despair creeping into his heart as surely as the cold crept into his bones as the sun began to sink again on the second day.

IT NEVER RAINS...

Few of them slept much in the temporary shelter of the garage unit. The wind whistled through the many gaps and shook the steel roller shutter with a thunderous noise which disturbed all but the deepest of sleepers. Despite her tiredness, Leah could not stop her mind from working overtime with the million and one thoughts rushing through her brain. Ticking them off mentally, she found herself attacking one problem at a time with logic as her weapon.

She worked through each aspect of her fears, creating solutions to problems, contingencies for eventualities, answers to questions. Her main difficulty was that she faced so many different issues that, unwillingly, her brain switched between topics with all the capriciousness of a hyperactive kitten.

Lying curled up in her sleeping bag with her head propped on her bag and her hand resting on her rifle, she gave up on trying to file away all of the worries and distress like the wind outside was blowing them around in her head and mixing them together irreparably.

Twisting over onto her back, she lay flat and tried to empty her mind of all cognitive thought. She found her brain in a void, but into that void from all sides like bodiless voices came creeping back those same fears and more. The anxiety leaked insidiously into her mind like water into a boat with a thousand small holes in its hull.

As her last attempt to try and sleep, she came out of her own mind and pushed her consciousness down into her toes. She worked upwards through her body, concentrating on each muscle in turn, and she willed it to become heavy as she felt herself sinking further and further into the thin comfort of her makeshift bed.

Sleep so nearly took her into its blissful embrace until the howling wind, in her state of flux between awake and not, transformed into the screams of people.

They wailed and begged her for help, but she could not move and felt powerless to stop whatever faceless terror persecuted those who relied on her. As the screaming built to a crescendo in her head, she jolted awake and let out a loud, strangled cry, a foul hybrid of anguish and rage.

Having startled those nearest her, she grumbled to herself as she gave up on any hope of rest and wriggled free of the sleeping bag to roll it up and stuff it angrily into her pack. Stepping carefully over the others in the back of the big truck, she jumped down from the tailgate to jar her ankle, as exhaustion had robbed her of her natural litheness. As though she hadn't enough to be unhappy about already, she took a glance to her left where the murky stream of shadowy moonlight piercing their metal burrow shone down on the swathed body of Jack.

The events of the last twenty-four hours washed over her again, and she replayed the attack over and over to find fault in her actions. She could not, but still felt that she held some responsibility.

Opening a bottle of water and jumping up slightly to sit on a raised workbench, she heard the click, click of Ash's claws as he walked stiffly over to her side having sensed she was up. She reached down to fuss the huge animal and saw the gaping yawn as he displayed his numerous sharp teeth. The terrifying effect of seeing the damage his jaws could do was offset somewhat by the ridiculous noise his yawn made.

She chuckled softly, finding some sense of joy in a shitty world, and the noise seemed to offend the dog, who now eyed her with a mildly reproving look. Ignoring Ash's delicate sensibilities, she glanced around at the hole they had burrowed into. The dank, dusty garage was actually a lucky find as far as things went nowadays, she admitted to herself.

Startled from her reverie by a noise from the corner, one hand instinctively reached for a weapon until the realisation hit her: she could hear a person crying.

Slipping down from the bench in silence, she walked with her habitual sense of stealth towards the noise, expecting to find Henry feeling sorry for himself. She was alarmed and instantly upset to find Marie tucked into a foetal position behind a large toolbox.

Marie was shivering with cold, as she was only wearing a T-shirt with her back pressed against the cold metal, and in the poor light from the moon, Leah could see her face wet with tears and her eyes puffy from the torment of crying. Saying nothing, Leah sank to her knees and wrapped her arms tightly around her as a parent would do to a distressed child. Unable to say anything, Marie just cried harder into her shoulder and squeezed her tight to pull her forward. Narrowly avoiding hitting her head as she fell onto Marie, Leah would not allow herself to let go of the woman. As she held on tight to her, she could only begin to imagine what she was feeling: Dan was missing, Jack was dead, Marie was pregnant with no way of knowing she could survive the condition, and they were low on supplies and on the run with little or no idea where they were heading.

All these fears were shared with Leah to a great extent, but the girl reminded herself silently that she wasn't the one carrying a potential death sentence in her womb. Not once in all the time she had known Marie had she seen her do much more than shoot a disapproving look or raise her voice. To find her in such a state as she was now, to see her almost catatonic with pain and emotion, brought Leah's focus to a whole new and until now undiscovered level.

She missed Dan too, but as much as she wanted to burst out in tears of solidarity and shared pain, they would not come. Her heart was steel. She wanted nothing more than for Dan to come strolling back into their lives with all the cockiness and sarcasm he brought with him. She longed to see his unintentionally arrogant face look at her and try to impart advice without sounding condescending.

She missed him so much it had numbed her to the pain it caused to think he could be gone.

As she held on tight to Marie, she vowed to get these people safely to the rendezvous point, to find Dan and reunite their dysfunctional family before they drove off into the sunset and found the answers to all of their prayers.

Until that day, however, until the time when they were safe and fed and warm and out of all danger, she would remain as hard and as sharp as her knives. She had to, not only for herself but for everyone. When she had discharged those duties, then and only then would she allow herself to cry like an overtired toddler who had been denied their wish.

She had no idea how long she had rocked Marie back and forth while she smoothed her hair and shushed her, but when the constricted blood flow in her legs threatened to cause more pain than discomfort, she had to force her arms away and stand. Reaching down to Marie to help her up, she was suddenly struck how much the powerful and enigmatic woman who organised them all so efficiently needed her right then; she had transcended to adulthood and now she was the protector.

Leading Marie gently back to the truck, Leah helped her into her sleeping bag and tucked her in, stroking her hair again until she passed out with exhaustion.

Backing away slowly, she stretched out her cramped muscles and returned to her perch on the workbench. Sensing that the moment of intimacy that he had not been invited to was over, Ash slunk from the shadows again to be at her side. The only indication of the big animal moving was the clacking of his claws, and Leah pondered the terror someone would feel being on the receiving end of Ash when he was engaged in business.

As the pre-dawn light began to seep through the few windows, she busied herself as quietly as possible preparing water on the few small camp cookers they had left and stacking a selection of foil packets at the side ready. When she had decided that the others had slept enough, she went round them all to shake them awake, taking a small and cruel bit of enjoyment in ending their sleep which she had not joined in with.

They ate breakfast in relative silence, and as though both were ignoring the events in the night by mutual agreement, Marie gave a subtle squeeze of thanks on her hand as she passed by. To try and assuage her tiredness, Leah drank a coffee so strong that she almost had to chew it.

Loading up the equipment into the truck in some sense of order, Neil climbed behind the wheel and turned the key.

Only to find the engine totally dead.

Neil tried over and over to start the big machine, his only reward being a ticking noise of struggling electrics. With a resigned sigh, he got out and propped open the large bonnet to look at the engine. The rest of them shuffled around, unsure what to do.

Leah sidled up to Neil, his hands already sporting an oily black residue as he poked and prodded at the cold engine components. She watched for a few seconds as he went through his curious personal form of logic and worked through the potential problems while he muttered under his breath and moved his hands as he spoke. Clearing her throat to bring him out of his thoughts, she asked what was wrong.

"Nothing I can't fix, and it's not like there aren't any tools lying around!" Neil answered with forced joviality, waving a hand over the dusty racks of toolboxes to explain his lack of concern.

Leaning closer with intense seriousness, she whispered close to his ear that they had to be at the rendezvous by the next dawn, meaning that he only had a matter of hours to rectify their lack of transport.

Nodding his understanding to her, he straightened up as Jimmy walked around the front of the engine, rolling up his sleeves to help.

Leaving the two men to talk about oil and other things she didn't understand, she went back to the others to try and think of something worthwhile for them to do while they waited. Finding that most had already found comfortable places to rest, she decided instead to talk to Mitch. Finding him resting with his eyes closed as he was propped up on a bed of bags, she sat down lightly next to him. They had a brief exchange about the engine not starting, to which Mitch expressed his faith in Neil's ability to fix the problem.

"I know, it's just that time is an issue," she told him.

"We'll get there and he will be waiting," the soldier assured her, realising that the girl was almost frantic on the inside at being separated from Dan. Reaching up to cuff her lightly on the head, he instantly regretted his decision as the pain in his bruised chest radiated throughout his body.

Changing the subject, Leah asked him about the grenade Jack had given him which had made their escape possible.

Mitch's face dropped and became a mask of neutrality.

"I don't want to talk about that," he said without emotion, but Leah was not one to be put off by grown men in a mood.

"Why?" she asked simply, unperturbed by the warning look he shot her in response.

He paused, unsure whether to unleash his thoughts about a man he counted as a friend and one who died trying to save them. In the end, his feelings ran too deep to hold his tongue. "Because I served in Northern Ireland. Because I saw people die from bombs and bullets. Because it's too hard to fight a war when you don't know who or where the enemy is when most people there are just trying to get on with their lives. Jack was one of them, and I'm not sure I can deal with that yet."

"Jack was one of us," she told him gently as she stood up, "and I'm going to bury him with the respect he deserves for who he was when I knew him, not what he did in the past."

~

Having gathered others to help, and informing Henry that he would need to dig a grave, she left the unit with Ash to find an appropriate spot nearby. Turning left away from the built-up area instead of right as she had the day before, she soon found a small public park where trees stood proudly as they shed their richly colourful autumnal leaves. Crouching in cover for a while before she was satisfied that the area was clear, she stood and returned to the garage.

Arriving back after a necessary detour an hour later, having found the necessary tools in a small hardware shop, she led a small band back to the park via the route she dictated to collect the spades she had left on the roadside.

Keeping watch over them all as Henry dug a hole in the earth, she saw how the boy threw himself into the task feverishly, as though his effort now could in some way make up for his foolish actions. She told herself that she would have to stop punishing him after this last enforced task; to continue to do so was unjust and made her feel unnecessarily cruel.

Marie had insisted on coming to say a few words, and as Jack's sleeping bag was lowered into the rectangular hole, she stood at the head and watched as the earth was piled on top of him. Unable to rouse herself to make a stirring speech, she merely shared a small recollection of something funny he had done once back at the house and asked others to share any similar stories. Ceremony over, they returned to the unit in a dutiful line following girl and dog.

Finding a filthy Neil engrossed in his work, he looked up startled when he saw she had returned. Holding a piece of machinery aloft with wires trailing from it, he declared that he had found the problem. Adam caught her eye, and walked over to tell her she should get some rest.

"I'm fine!" she argued.

"You look like shit," he answered. "Try to sleep for a bit." No longer able to mount a sufficient defence through exhaustion, she nodded her acceptance and found a quiet corner to tuck herself away in. As Ash joined her and circled four times on the spot to be sure he had chosen the right place, he lay half across her legs and began to snore gently within minutes.

Finally able to rest, she closed her eyes and slept.

She was woken only a few hours later by the unmistakable roar of a big diesel engine barking into life. Throwing off the sleeping dog, she climbed free of her comfort and walked to Neil to receive the offer of an oil-covered high five.

"Let's go, people. We can make it there by nightfall if we hurry," she called to them, seeing smiles of hope returned to her.

OUTNUMBERED

Dan sat in the same position until the sun had set, then returned to the back of the Land Rover to sleep during the dark hours.

As he lay awake throughout most of the night, his thoughts raged through a torrent of different possibilities and none of them were good. The agreement was to wait until the following dawn before falling back to the secondary meeting point. Were they already there? Had they skipped the bridge and gone straight to ERV two? Had they been captured?

He had to stick to the plan, and if they didn't turn up at the next spot, then he would return to the beginning of the trail and would not stop until he either found them or died, whichever came first.

As the first indication of an impending dawn showed on the distant skyline, he emerged from the dark interior to prepare for the last day on the bridge before the window to meet there expired. Repeating the process of the day before, he ate breakfast and sat up to watch forlornly at the end of the bridge.

As midday approached, his anxiety forced him into some kind of action to preserve what little he had left of his sanity. Walking towards the few buildings in sight, he cleared each room in turn but found little of use anywhere. Strolling lazily back to his vehicle, he ate again and cherished one of his last few cigarettes. He only had six left in the packet, and he worked through the mental arithmetic to ration one per every block of hours until the others would join him.

Unable to stick to his self-imposed quota, he was down to the last two long before the sun began its descent. Glancing disconsolately at the sky, his breath stopped in his throat as his brain registered movement ahead of him.

Desperate to respond to a potential threat but fighting an inner battle with himself, he calmly climbed down from his vantage point and stretched his back. To anyone watching, he would appear like he had seen nothing.

At least he hoped it would.

Out of sight from whoever or whatever was to his front, he threw all of his equipment in the back and prepared himself for contact; he checked his magazines were accessible and tightened his vest ready for something, even if he didn't know what it would be. Walking carefully along the side of the vehicle, he raised the carbine and pointed the scope towards the end of the bridge where he hoped his friends would be coming from.

It wasn't them. They wouldn't be sneaking between the sparse cover and moving forwards at a crouch to try and remain undetected. Now they were closer and he could make out details, he could see that armed men were heading in his direction.

Thinking as fast as he could, his only sensible course of action would be to get behind the wheel and drive away. A glance behind him told a different story, as he could make out at least three shapes coming low towards him from that direction.

Feeling stupid and exposed, he decided that his only option was to fight. He had a foreboding sense that it was a fight he might not win, and decided that he had little to lose, so reached into the cab and grabbed the radio mic.

"On the bridge. ERV one. Armed hostiles—" he managed before the first shot screamed over his head. Dropping the mic and retreating from the shot, he knelt and took aim at the attackers to his rear, who were still not in a position to take cover and fire at him. Controlling his breathing and trying to ignore the shouts and gunshots from behind, he aimed and squeezed the trigger in a few short bursts.

Dropping one of them to lie still on the tarmac, two more turned and fled out of range, terrified and appalled by his accuracy.

Too late: he took his eye away from the scope to deal with the ones coming from the front just as a bellowed challenge sounded over his left shoulder. A bearded man swung a full-size axe at his head from less than a pace away. He could see it happening and felt powerless to do anything but accept the brutal ending.

His body overrode the decisions his mind was making.

In an instinctive flinch reaction, he fell back to the ground and raised the rifle just in time to deflect the vicious blow. The sharpened blade of the axe hit the ejection port of his M4 and mangled the metal, rendering the gun eternally useless. He dropped it and scrabbled backwards on the ground as he tried uselessly to free his sidearm from the holster on his vest but finding that he could not do it without halting his desperate retreat. Drawing the shotgun over his shoulder was even more of an impossibility, so he switched tactics and decided to fight animal on animal.

Launching himself back towards the axeman, Dan raised a boot and stamped out into his straight leg, forcing the knee backwards with a sickening crunch. He didn't hear the man's screams as he dropped to his back, only saw the axe which he picked up and reversed to end the man who had tried to kill him.

Raising the weapon high in the air, he looked down, expecting to see fear in his intended victim's eyes as he knew his death was imminent, but instead he only saw his attention was drawn away from the weapon searing towards his face.

Realising too late that he had lost, Dan glanced over his right shoulder.

And looked straight into the butt of the rifle which, swung like a club with terrible accuracy, knocked him unconscious.

FIGHT CLUB

Three days of the same routine followed where Steve was left alone with the exception of his twice-daily visits to deliver food and issue medication. Only once more did he see Alice, and as before, he was careful to avoid the guard gaining any sense that the two colluded in any way.

On the fourth morning, he woke to find a familiar face sitting in the corner reading a book. Only the face was unfamiliar at the same time: his right eye was barely open and the livid purple bruising extended over his freshly broken nose where it began to haze yellow at the fringes of the injury. Despite the severe trauma evident, the eyes sparkled and the mouth showed a wide grin.

Stiffly, Jan rose to his feet and began the morning routine of checking Steve's injuries and vital statistics. The crippled pilot was so grateful to see Jan back that he was struck dumb and simply stared at his face waiting for an explanation.

"Tell me!" he whispered, prompting a further grin from the big South African.

"OK," he said, trying to calm Steve's excitement. "Sit back and relax, because this is one hell of a story."

After days of subtle hints and words in the ears of the right guards, Jan had managed to beg an invitation to the camp's illicit sporting activity. It was an underground movement, not endorsed by the hierarchy but no doubt not discouraged either, as Richards would certainly know of its existence.

A whispered buzz ran around after each event, but nobody yet spoke of it openly for fear of interrogation for their indiscretions. Jan had finally received the invitation he was after and would fight his first bout that night.

Unfortunately, he had no way of letting Steve know that he had got in, as the summons to participate was an immediate one. He was led away in the clothes he wore, his usual green scrubs, and taken to the arena which had been fashioned from yet more shipping containers, one of which served as the entrance and exit for the fighters, positioned together to form a hexagonal pit of dry earth. The grass which had previously grown there was killed off long ago by the barbaric activities the ground saw. Muted cheers echoed around the pit, as one fight was already underway and the crowd seemed to be enjoying themselves at the spectacle.

Told to remove his shoes and shirt, he was ushered through a metal door to wait in the dark for his turn. Being deprived of his sense of sight only served to accentuate the noises he could hear: the smacking of meat, like a butcher tenderising a large joint, mixed with the hushed reactions of the crowd as the battle raged on just outside his thin metal safety bubble. He jumped in fright at the sudden sound as the fighters crashed heavily into the wall of his container and shook the steel as the grunts and impacts resonated through to his ears. Bouncing on the spot and loosening his muscles for what was to come, he cricked his neck from side to side to receive the rewards of the popping sounds as his ligaments snapped into place.

He was focused, but he was scared. He was confident in his own abilities, but facing an unknown opponent was a dangerous act. Hearing the crowd's mood switch from bloodthirsty glee to jeering disappointment, he knew his turn was up soon.

Winner stays on, he had been told, so that meant that his adversary would be tired from beating the last failed gladiator. There were no rules, he had been told, so it was a raw gutter fight until he lost. The only unspoken law was that he shouldn't intentionally kill anyone, and hoped that the same went for whoever he faced. Only one death had occurred here, and it had been hurriedly covered up to prevent word reaching any further.

Screeching metal and the sudden invasion of light into his world as the single door to the pit swung open announced his turn to step inside.

Blinking as he went, he looked up to see that the tops of the containers which prevented his escape were thronged with people. Most were guards, but he recognised faces of others among the mob. Cooks, cleaners, farmers, all packed together to watch one man beat another to a pulp for enjoyment.

Standing aside as the last contender was carried unconscious back to where he had emerged from, he took one last look at the baying crowd before focusing his attention on his foe.

He could never tell them apart, but he faced one of the brothers who had bragged so loudly about how they had infiltrated Steve's home and took them down without a fight. He believed the rumours that this man was one of Richards's trusted elite – one of the balaclava-clad bastards who flanked him everywhere he went – and Jan began to suspect that he was in for some pain.

Stick to the plan, he told himself.

He was taller than Jan by half a head at least, and his long, sinewy arms spoke of a strength which wasn't overtly obvious in his size. Having seen the state of the man carried out, Jan weighed up the damage to his enemy and saw a remarkable difference; it did not appear to have been a fair fight.

Jan knew his capabilities, although he had not fought anyone in a long time, and he had to be certain to lose this fight while tempting his opponent sufficiently to want to fight him again.

He had to lose, but he had to hurt the pompous victor in front of him and give him enough cause to feel affronted. After all, what warrior wanted to go down to a nurse?

Glancing up again, he could see people wagering goods in trade on the result of the fight, and he was saddened that they would win those bets because he had no intention of fighting more than a single round that night. Instead, he intended to get the full measure of the champion, secure his place in the running order, and learn as much as he could while trying to stay alive.

Having finally noticed Jan in front of him, the sweating man held his hands up to the crowd and gestured for them to join in his mockery of an unworthy opponent.

Up close, Jan decided that this was most probably Will, not that it mattered. Shrugging, Will ran towards Jan without warning and launched his first attack.

Stopping short of him and throwing punches in bunches with his left and his right, Jan ducked aside of both blows and lowered his body weight only to receive the impact of a knee to the flesh just above his hip as the combo was followed up. Staggering backwards, he sucked in a large gulp of air and hoped he had not been winded yet. Finding that his diaphragm wasn't spasming, he took a stance and advanced forward.

His opponent waited for him, waving for the crowd to cheer, then suddenly whipped out an inside leg kick to Jan's thigh, following immediately with a kick to his head, which he blocked with ease but knew that this wasn't the real attack. Stepping back and putting most of his weight on his back foot, the expected sweep of the taller man's foot glanced off his own ankle without sufficient power to fell him.

A flash of eye contact between them let Jan know that he had angered Will, and no doubt he intended to exact revenge on him for ruining one of his most crowd-pleasing moves.

Determined to knock the South African to the ground and raise his standing among his followers, Will advanced again with more care and began to test Jan's guard by attacking low and high. Jan was happy to let this happen as he fended off blows which lacked the power to do any real damage; the longer Will showboated for the crowd, the more he learned about him.

Shuffling backwards and circling left and right, Jan let him come at him time and again as he deflected each attack to try and frustrate his opponent. Whether it was immaturity or sheer arrogance, Will's patience cracked sooner than expected and he launched into a reckless assault.

Sensing his moment was now, Jan took two steps back to invite the spinning back kick he was anticipating, and when the attack started, he retraced those two steps fast and shot in close to clinch him; trapping Will's outside leg with his own, he slammed him to the ground hard and rose to throw three big punches to his head. Allowing his arm to be blocked on the next attack, he went with the impetus as Will lifted his hips to throw Jan clear. He rolled away and rose to his feet smoothly to turn and face the threat.

The crowd erupted with screaming and cheering; for once, they might have a real fight to watch.

Watching Will get to his feet and dust himself off, the mixture of surprise and rage in his eyes made the nurse absolutely certain that he was going to experience a significant amount of pain that night, but he reminded himself that it was necessary in order for the plan to work. Coming forward with more caution, Will switched his approach and came in low for a series of body shots which Jan tucked up to receive, only to have him switch tactics again and spring backwards to deliver a big sweeping leg kick to his left side just below the knee.

Involuntarily dropping his hands towards the source of the immediate pain and numbness, Jan suffered a follow-up kick to the right eye as Will moved effortlessly between attacks. Jan felt dizzy as his brain's direction had been so savagely reversed.

Staggering away to regroup, he now knew that Will was dangerous, and that he had tricks up his sleeve. Jan had more than a few of his own, but this wasn't the time to show them. He had to get in a few lucky shots, knock the bastard down, then take the beating he was due and lose. That was the plan, and as much as he wanted to break the egotistical prick in front of him, he had to wait.

Twice more Will came at him, and twice more his attacks switched violently between close quarters and long-range kicks. Both times, Jan sucked up the punishment and stayed resolutely on his feet.

As the next kick came at his head, Jan abandoned the guard and instead stepped in hard to lift Will under his raised leg and pitch him savagely into the dirt once more. Will reacted well, rolling his head to take the impact on his shoulders and countered with an immediate attempt to lock up Jan's left arm.

Suffering a break or a dislocation could be fatal to the plan, and Jan wriggled out of the attempted counter with one of his own as he stood squarely on Will's chest and spun to roll away.

Having demonstrated that he too was dangerous, Jan began the next attack with feigned excitement to see how the younger man fared in defence. Swinging big hits at his head and his body and throwing kicks at his legs showed that Will was fast, very fast, and at every chance, he looked for a counterattacking opportunity.

Jan could feel the breath burning hot and fast in his throat now, and knew that he wasn't going to be there for much longer. Stepping back to encourage Will to attack him again, he allowed himself to produce just one of his favourite go-to moves. Allowing Will to make contact with a combo, he waited for the inevitable big finish and prepared himself. As Will's footwork changed to provide room for the big swinging kick which would no doubt finish his opponent, Jan took a quick step back, leaning away, and watched in slow motion as the kick sailed through thin air.

With no great impact to slow his body, Will continued to spin forwards off balance and straight into the loving embrace of Jan.

Delivering a brutal haymaker of a right hook, he caught Will directly under the ribs and followed with a short-arm elbow strike to the head with his left.

With a sickening noise, Will went down and a stunned silence descended on the arena. The champion had never gone down during a fight. Rumour had it that the only person who could beat him was his brother, but the two vowed never to fight one another so the theory remained untested. Now they had watched a nobody, a nurse, fell him like a slaughtered animal.

Hoping that he hadn't hit him too hard, Jan stepped back and shouted at Will to get up. Shaking on unsteady legs, he did. Wiping blood from the corner of his right eye where Jan's elbow had split the skin, he fixed this upstart challenger with a look of such hatred and malevolence that Jan quailed and took an involuntary step backwards.

Will would have to hurt him now, not because he drew blood or fought back too hard, but because the crowd were no longer chanting for him. Stepping forward to renew their faith in him, he went to work on Jan.

Sitting back with an incredulous look in his eye, he watched the face of the grinning South African and marvelled at his strength and resolve. How anyone could be so happy to have been beaten up so badly that they were bed-bound for three days was beyond even his ability to understand, but here he was, and he seemed thoroughly pleased with himself.

When his shock subsided, Steve realised he too was very happy. Very happy indeed. They had successfully infiltrated the underground fight club, which would prove to be a very powerful tool in the bid to eventually overthrow Richards – as long as Jan didn't get himself killed in the meantime.

"When will you have to fight again?" Steve asked with concern, not only for Jan's life but for the timeline of their plan.

"Probably three weeks. They only do it the first Friday in every month because there aren't many fighters and people need to heal," Jan answered with a shrug, unconcerned at the prospect of facing more physical punishment which could jeopardise his life and health.

Steve mulled this over as he chewed his lip. "Just don't, for fuck's sake, get yourself killed or badly hurt," he said with genuine feeling.

"You leave that to me!" Jan answered with a smug grin. "Because next month, I'm challenging the other one of those bastards, and he'll learn not to mess with a Springbok too."

Steve was infected by his battered friend's enthusiasm, and felt his own face cracking into a smile at the thought of the other "twin" receiving some treatment the likes of which he enjoyed dishing out but was unlikely to enjoy taking.

Fixing the South African's gaze intensely, he reached out and gripped his shoulder tight. "Thank you, my friend. Thank you."

"Don't thank me yet! Ja doos!" he answered with a muted chuckle, making Steve believe that he had just suffered a good-natured but unpleasant insult.

"I mean it," he insisted with a smile. "Stay alive and in one bloody piece, but promise me that when the time comes, you'll hurt them both, badly, and then we can rid this damned place of people like that."

Smirking with a confidence that made Steve believe him, Jan answered, "Trust me, when the time comes I'll kill the pair of them with my bare hands. But first, you need to be strong enough to take over and kill Richards after I've taken out his little sidekicks."

With that, they began their more intense but secret routine of physiotherapy.

NOTHING TO LOSE

He woke with a start, trying to make sense of the last few moments before he lost consciousness. He had no idea how long he had been out, but he knew as the feeling returned to the rest of his body that he had his hands bound together and was blindfolded.

Bastards, he thought savagely, wishing he could rip off his bindings and kill them all. Only he was tied tightly, and when he tried to move his feet, he found them pinned together also. Reaching awkwardly down, he felt the same rough twine cutting into his swelling flesh as was holding his wrists tightly together. Using his thumbs, he forced the stinking rag used to cover his eyes up only to find that he was in a windowless room with the only light source being a glow around the doorframe which showed the swirling dust. Realising that he felt cold, he looked down to find that he had been stripped and was wearing only his boxer shorts as he lay down on the cold floor of the store cupboard he inhabited.

For that, he thought, he was really going to hurt someone.

Forcing himself to conduct a thorough top-to-toe survey, as he had unfortunately had cause to do so many times before, he found that his only real problem was the major pain in the right side of his jaw where his head had been smacked out of the park as though the bastard wielding the gun had been aiming for a home run.

Moving his neck gently, he felt no grating or pain in his upper spine and resigned himself in relative comfort to the fact that it seemed to be just another concussion. At that point, the thought struck him that Kate would be furious with him for collecting yet another serious head injury; if he were a professional boxer, he would have been medically retired by now.

Pushing away all thoughts of the others or of any pain and self-sympathy, he began to analyse his surroundings and decipher their clues to find a way out of the mess he was in.

He had to get free. He had to get to the others at the second rendezvous point. He would very much like to get his gear and clothes back and kill a few of the bastards who had tied him up, but there were always secondary and primary problems to solve.

Shuffling over to the shaft of light coming from the doorframe, he put his scarred eye then his left ear to it to find out any information that could aid in his escape and retribution.

Fearing that he may be doomed with poor luck that day, the door swung open and cracked him heavily on the left side of his face to knock him back hard to the ground as someone walked in. Their surprise at not finding him unconscious quickly turned into mirth as they realised they had just inadvertently clocked him again.

Rolling on the floor as the men in the doorway laughed among themselves did nothing to help his mood as he foolishly looked up to make eye contact with one. The look of pure violent malevolence he gave was sufficient to earn him a hard kick to the ribs.

Dan scribbled another mental note, this time to wait until you're untied before you pick a fight.

The other men disappeared as he gasped for air, bathing him in sunlight, only for one to return with a single chair and sit on it directly in front of where he lay. The man sat lazily, leaning down to eye him closely with a cruel but amused grin. Sitting back and toying with a packet of cigarettes, he continued to smirk at him. His languid style made Dan burn with anger and he allowed himself to drift off and imagine what it would feel like to punch him in the throat and watch him choke. The thought made him smile, and that smile seemed to amuse the man watching him.

"My name is Leo," he said in near-perfect English, "but my men call me 'le chasseur'."

He smiled and relaxed further, sinking into his seat as he produced one of the two remaining cigarettes from the pack and lit it, taking his time as he pocketed the lighter and inhaled slowly.

"Chasseur: do you know what this means, Englishman?" he asked threateningly.

Dan had an idea, but realising that the bastard was sitting there smoking fifty per cent of all the cigarettes he had left in the world made him tight-lipped and insolent.

Smiling, Leo told him anyway. "It means 'hunter'. You understand me OK, Englishman? Is my accent too strong for you to hear my words?" he said mockingly, inhaling again and blowing a lazy smoke ring over Dan's head. "I am a hunter of men," he said with a hint of steel in his voice, "but you were the first of many to give me, how you might say, a challenge." He relished the last word with a wolfish smile.

In that instant, Dan recognised him for what he was: another bloody madman intent on forcing his will on others.

Deciding that he had nothing important to say yet, Dan held his tongue and just watched the Frenchman smoke his cigarette. Leo regarded him with humour, an arrogant and superior humour as though Dan were an amusement or a mere insignificance in his life.

"So now you will tell me where your camp is, where your people are and what you have for us," he growled at him as he leant in close. Taking another drag on the cigarette and holding the glowing tip close to Dan's eyes, he blew a slow stream of smoke directly into his captive's eyes as a smile crept over his face. Leaning to the side as though he were avoiding the stinging smoke, Dan glanced through the open door to find that Leo seemed to feel comfortable enough to have this small tête-à-tête alone.

Fool, thought Dan.

Striking like a snake, he wrapped his bound hands over the hunter's head and brought it down with a sickening crunch onto his upright kneecap. The single blow was sufficient to render the man instantly useless, and Dan was actually grateful for the warmth that the sudden gush of blood from the broken nose gave him. Leo was down and out, and he hadn't uttered a sound. Leaning around to look out of the door, Dan breathed out in relief that the crunching noise hadn't alerted a single one of the others to his sudden escape attempt. Going back to the unconscious man on the floor, he found a knife on his belt and used it to cut his bonds quickly.

Searching the rest of his pockets, Dan tucked his last cigarette and lighter into the waistband of his underwear; there was no way he was going to give up on that small pleasure.

Hovering in the shadows of the doorway, Dan watched for any sign of anyone responding to the small noises his actions had caused, but found none. Glancing once at the sleeping Leo, he decided that it was unwise to leave anyone – even one who merely claimed to be capable – alive to follow him. It just seemed like a bad business model.

As he bent down to carefully insert the sharp knife into the hunter's femoral artery, a bellowed challenge erupted from behind him. Spinning around to find another man wide-eyed with shock silhouetted in the doorway, he drove the blade forward unthinkingly, into his chest. The blade initially grated on bone, then found easier passage between the ribs as the sharp tip sought the path of least resistance and slid neatly into the chest cavity of his newest enemy.

The shock in the man's eyes turned to utter horror as he realised that he was effectively dying, even though the pain hadn't yet hit him fully.

Retracting the knife before the muscles went into spasm and threatened to hold the blade tight, Dan gave a slight twist and withdrew it before another target came into play. The shout must have alerted others, and from Dan's hazy recollection, there had to be at least three more to deal with.

Staggering from the room as the head injury still impaired him greatly, he went in search of his personal effects; God only knew how much he needed his evil, stubby shotgun right then.

As he bounced between office furniture through the open-plan room he found himself in, his thoughts drifted off to Ash. If he had him there now, he would feel almost invincible. As his knees gave out on him for the first time, he felt the incredible pressure build in his damaged head as a wave of dizziness threatened to overcome him.

Moving with murderous and reckless abandon from room to room, he burst open through each door in turn, wearing only underwear and a bloodstain to accompany the knife in his hand and the grimace on his face. Behind the third door, he found a suddenly shocked and equally embarrassed man trying on his ballistic vest complete with his own Walther still in the holster.

The two men froze as they both stared at each other for a second. It suddenly became a race of who could bring a weapon to bear first, and as the terrified Frenchman scrabbled backwards as he attempted in vain to pull the sidearm free from the vest, Dan pounced on him, pinning him to the floor with his knees on the man's chest. Leaning close to his face with his left forearm pressed painfully on his windpipe, Dan grinned at him malevolently.

"You've got to twist the barrel to draw it smoothly, see?" he said as he slipped the gun free with a practised turn of his wrist. Placing the end of the short suppressor hard under the chin of the man stranded under his body weight, he grinned maniacally at him as his victim babbled incoherently in high-speed French.

"Je ne comprends pas," Dan said nastily in his worst French accent as he pulled the trigger and fountained the man's brains up the white plasterboard in front of him. The spray of atomised blood and brain matter splashed back over his own face, making him spit out the fragments which had gone in his mouth inadvertently. Working fast to strip the man of his own equipment as well as his trousers, he felt a little less ridiculous, as he was no longer running around an office building murdering men in his underwear.

Shrugging himself into the vest and trousers, which were slightly too big for him in the waist, he continued to stalk the rooms barefoot for any others. The wanton feeling that he had to recover all of his gear pushed him on, room to room, until he discovered his shotgun on a table with the boxed supplies which had previously been in the back of his Land Rover. As he looked through his rifled equipment on

211

the desk, he heard and felt the simultaneous blast of a shotgun being fired from close range. Falling to the floor, he felt the stinging sensation mixing with the trickle of fresh, warm blood as some of the pellets had infiltrated his body where the vest had not absorbed their impact. Spinning around, he brought the ungainly shotgun to bear and selected a target: from that range, he could not miss, even though his enemy had failed to kill him from the same distance, and he fired to lift the man clean off his feet and throw him backwards in bloody ruin. Deciding that he had suffered enough attention from these people, he limped and staggered to the doorway and outside to freedom.

Only to be met at gunpoint by two more men. Dropping to his knees, he decided that he had fought enough and killed enough of them to justify his surrender and imminent death now.

"Do it, you fucking prick," he said in a slur, smiling up at the man pointing a barrel in his face. *Fuck the lot of them*, he thought as he closed his eyes and waited for the end.

~

Two meaty thuds followed by grunts and the sound of men collapsing to the floor made him open his eyes again and question if he was still alive.

Seeing Leah emerge at a crouch from behind a nearby commercial trash bin with her weapon raised made him certain that he had died and was now imagining things.

Staring with unbelieving eyes at Ash streaking forwards toward him made him absolutely sure that he had rapidly transcended to the afterlife and was now joined by his greatest loves. Pitching forwards, he finally let the adrenaline and the concussion take him into unconsciousness as he landed hard on the concrete.

The dog whined and licked desperately at the blood on his face, fearing that it was his and not that of the men he had killed.

IT WOULD TAKE TOO LONG TO EX-PLAIN

Leah almost whipped the group to make them move faster. No sooner had her foggy brain understood the meaning of the sound of the engine did she spark into life herself; her own power output would have a relatively higher brake horsepower if the measure were taken, and the others found themselves harried and harangued into action.

Firing the oily and exhausted Neil into action, he turned to Jimmy, who immediately offered to drive the big truck. Ripping her hands on the rusty chain as she tore at the mechanism to raise the shutter doors with a feverish excitement, she was the last to hop aboard the vehicle as they made their way with all haste to the rendezvous point.

Mitch, although physically impaired, had figured they should make the meeting place with an hour of daylight to spare, and from there they could regroup and decide where to go. The concept that Dan might not be there was an unspeakable thing, and although some may have suspected it, it was not an opinion anyone wished to offer.

When they were about an hour away from the bridge's location, the radio crackled into sudden life in the cab.

The burst of static relayed two distinct words: Bridge. Hostiles.

Glancing between themselves, Jimmy, Neil and Leah said nothing, but Jimmy pressed his right foot down a little harder.

Fifty minutes later, they slowed their approach as the start of the bridge came into sight. Leah instructed Jimmy to stop and wait as she skipped ahead with Ash at her heel. Although it was agonising for the others, she kept still for over ten minutes as she scanned every single inch of the ground she could see.

No sign of Dan.

The only thing to catch her eye was a glint of something reflected about one hundred yards onto the bridge.

Turning and indicating with a flat hand for the others in the truck to hold their position, she stalked forward with the dog at her side until she reached the place where the reflection originated.

Bending to one knee, she picked up one of a dozen bullet casings scattered on the rough concrete on the roadway. Picking one up, she sniffed it and recoiled as the fresh stench of cordite stung her nostrils.

There had been a gun battle here; someone had fired rounds recently, rounds which were the same calibre as her own weapon, and now there was no trace of them. Moving her search out a few feet from the empty casings, she found a small patch of dark road. Touching it with her fingers, the tips came back with a faint red. Blood. Nowhere near enough to indicate that anyone had died there, but enough to mean that this wasn't just a paper cut.

Combined with the recently fired casings, her heart sank as she thought that they were too late.

Turning and jogging back to the others on the truck, she thought about how to share the potentially bad news with the others, especially Marie, as she was delicate enough about Dan's missing status as it was, and she didn't even know about the radio transmission yet.

Taking matters into her own hands, more to negate the moaning objections of the others if they knew what she planned, she told them to sit tight while she scouted around. Neil began to interject until the girl less than a third of his age silenced him.

"If you think any of us but Adam can keep up with me and Ash, then fine, but you can't. And Adam is the fittest one here who can still use his weapon, so stop telling me what to do, Grandad."

With that, she turned her back and stalked away, appalled at her own blatant rudeness to a man she held a huge amount of love and respect for. She told herself that the rudeness was a necessary ruse to prevent him coming after her, and that in her own way she was protecting him from getting involved in whatever trouble she was intending to find.

Come hell or high water, she was going to find Dan. Even if that meant wading through a dozen bodies which she had personally converted from alive to dead, and even if it meant hauling his dead body with her, she was bloody well bringing him back.

Standing on the roof of a wrecked car, she scanned the area for anywhere she thought he could be. Using her best guess, she headed for a building which she thought looked defensible with Ash in faithful tow.

~

Rounding a corner, she froze at some form of noisy commotion inside the building ahead. Hearing that commotion become two shotgun blasts made her heart race, and as she pressed forwards, that terror deep in her chest became a sudden weeping delight as she saw movement through the dirty glass window ahead. A flash of familiarity, a desperate hope that she had recognised him.

It was all she could do not to cry out Dan's name and run forwards, but the undeniable sense of self-preservation ingrained in her every waking thought by Dan and Steve made her hesitate in caution.

That hesitation gave her the split-second advantage which saved both of their lives.

Two men emerged from cover just as Dan burst into the outside world. He dropped to his knees and said something to them, just as she rose and slotted a single bullet neatly into the head of each man threatening her adoptive father.

As both slumped lifelessly around him, she moved forwards at the ready, gun up and tracking for anyone else who wanted to take on her family. Ash streaked ahead to his master and began to fuss him. Glancing down briefly from the holographic sights of her gun, she saw that Dan was hurt. He barely seemed awake and he was definitely injured as blood began to pool around his knees.

Deciding that their immediate withdrawal was more important than anything else, she slung the rifle on her back and hauled Dan to his feet with his arm over her shoulder. Dragging him back into cover, she once again scanned the building but found nobody willing or able to come forward and challenge them. Dan muttered incoherently and tried to move but instead floundered like a drunk. Gently taking the Walther from his hand, she returned it to the holster and used the tough carry handle at the collar of his vest to drag him back towards the truck and more relative safety.

Exhausted, she had to leave him barely conscious a few hundred metres from the others and run back for help in recovering him.

Hearing a shout from her right made her freeze. Turning, she saw a man with a fearsome beard holding a rifle at his hip as he walked towards her. Holding up her hands and saying nothing, she backpedalled to entice the man further forward.

"Arrêtez," he growled at her, only to realise his mistake in emerging too far into the open. Hearing a ripping snarl coming from his left, he was powerless to do anything as Ash advanced on him menacingly. Switching his glance from Leah to Ash, he hesitated, as he couldn't decide who to aim the gun at first. Deciding to shoot the girl, he twitched the gun towards her just as Ash pounced forward and sank his teeth into the exposed flesh of his left arm.

Dropping the gun in agony, he died with a single bullet in his forehead fired by Leah.

"Good boy," she told Ash, breathless from the adrenaline before she turned and ran towards the truck for help.

Adam moved without hesitation, and when he reached Dan, he hauled him with ease onto his shoulders and carried him at a trot back to Kate.

The shouts and screams of shock, fear, delight and a mix of other feelings drowned out what Kate was trying to say to her.

Leah simply shook her head and told her to fix him before climbing back into the cab and telling Jimmy to get his foot down. Her last glimpse of Dan was seeing him with a lopsided smile as he tried in vain with no hand–eye coordination to light a single crumpled cigarette.

They had to get clear of the bridge before more men came for them.

THE LONG AND BORING ROAD

The four of them in the Land Rover felt stagnant. They had been travelling for what felt like days on the same empty stretch of concrete monotony, despite the excitement of seeing a severed head. Paul and Chris both slept in the back, more out of disinterest than of tiredness, and while Lexi kept the vehicle going in a straight line, even Simon at her side began to flag.

Another fifty minutes down the same dull road, they came to the interesting break of a long-abandoned tollgate. When Lexi had last visited the country, each of the booths held a person who could at least smile and bid a hello even if there was no common language between the driving and stationary parties. In more recent years, all of these booths had become automated for either cash or card, and as with everything in life, the human touch was being lost to a world where technology made a smile to a stranger a useless commodity with no tangible worth.

Lamenting this loss of human interaction and likening it sadly to her own life, Lexi rolled towards the blockage without much sense of awareness as her wandering mind was distracted.

As she slowed to negotiate the only unobstructed lane, she realised too late that she had fallen for a simple funnel trap. As both front tyres blew out simultaneously, the loud noise waking the other three occupants, so did the haunting and terrifying noise start from the woodland either side of the road.

A haunting howl rippled through the trees, issued from unseen mouths and indicating unspeakable things. She faced a choice: go forwards and blow out the back tyres on whatever hidden trap she had sprung or go back and find an alternative route with two flat tyres and no sure escape route. Realising too late that she may have condemned them all, she looked wildly from left to right as shapes began to emerge from the foliage.

One of those shapes stood clearly in the sunlight and turned her face to the sky to let out an animalistic howling noise. From all around them, the noise was echoed and amplified until the very air became a never-ending howl.

Forcing herself to be calm, she looked at the woman who instigated the foul and terrifying noise. Seeing that she was only armed with a sharpened stick in the form of a crude spear, she selected a third choice.

Fight them.

REGROUP

Sweating and out of breath from having dragged Dan to the truck, Leah regained her seat in the cab and made an executive decision.

"Get us back to the garage," she told Jimmy. He needed no further encouragement to be well away from the area and turned a wide circle to drive as instructed.

Leah could hear noises in the back as Kate tried to rouse Dan from his stupor and was no doubt cursing him for again using his head to deflect blows. The girl was tense throughout the relatively short journey; at least it felt much shorter than the agonising drive there when she was unsure if Dan was still alive.

Arriving back at the stiff metal shutters some time later, she jumped out and lowered the noisy doors with as much care as possible. Catching Adam's eye and pointing towards the biggest window, he nodded his assent to keep watch. Pacing towards the truck, she could hear Kate's loud and authoritative voice instructing everyone to get out of her way and leave her to work as she began the in-depth process of fixing Dan.

Seeing Henry shuffle past her, averting his eyes, she noticed that he still held Jack's pump-action, although he tried to shield it from her with his body.

Stepping in front of him, she almost snatched the weapon from his hand but stopped herself. "If you want to keep that, do something useful. Go and keep watch with Adam and do what he says," she said acidly while trying in vain to remove at least some of the scorn from her voice.

Overjoyed at the interaction between them, despite her obvious hostility, Henry beamed at her and skipped away to do as he was told. At least that kept him out of her way and away from Dan until she could break the news of Jack's death and the part that the boy played in it.

Reaching the open tailgate of the truck, she saw that only Marie, Sera and Kate remained as they tried to make Dan comfortable. Mitch stayed inside too, but his presence was tolerated, as moving was simply too painful for him yet, and the bouncing journey had exhausted him.

Leah cleared her throat, prompting Kate to turn. The annoyance on her face at the interruption melted away as she saw the girl, and knowing that she had put her life at risk to rescue Dan, she decided that Leah deserved an explanation.

"He's out of it, and all we can do is wait for him to wake up. It's another concussion." Her indignation about Dan's propensity for serious head injuries was evident. "And there seems to be plenty of shot to pick out of his..." she waved a hand vaguely over Dan's backside, not wanting to use the word she intended in front of Leah.

Kate's feelings of uselessness at not having the proper equipment to correctly diagnose him cut her deeply. She always tried to explain away her inabilities to perform magic, even though nobody had ever questioned her skill.

Nodding her understanding, Leah turned to make sure everyone else was gainfully employed and not in need of instruction, more for her own sanity than theirs, but Marie called her name. Turning back, she saw the pregnant woman struggle to her feet and stand still for a few seconds until her stiff legs began to work again before stepping carefully over bags and boxes to the rear of the truck. Taking her time with Leah's help to climb down safely, she wrapped the girl up in a huge hug and squashed her equipment painfully into her ribs. Marie would not let go, and kept repeating the same words over and over into her ear.

"Thank you."

It took until the following morning before Dan woke. The first sign of it happening was an excited yap from Ash as he slobbered over his master's face with undisguised joy. Others crowded around the open back of the truck as Kate pushed her way through the gathering throng to admonish the onlookers.

"Enough rubbernecking!" she snapped. "Give him some bloody air!"

Melting away to a more respectable distance, the group loitered at the fringes, hoping to snatch any snippet of news they could. As Dan tried to get up, he was instructed strictly not to try and move until their paramedic could conduct a more thorough assessment of his injuries.

"Right, tell me where it hurts," Kate said in a deliberately patronising tone, smiling.

"Everywhere," Dan moaned.

"Stop being a baby," Kate told him unsympathetically, "and be specific."

Closing his eyes and breathing through the pain, he started his own internal assessment and reported back as efficiently as his clouded brain could manage.

"Head. Right side. Someone smacked me with a rifle butt," he said before pausing and sending his consciousness lower. "Left side. Ribs. I think someone was practising their field goals on me…" He couldn't think of anywhere else specific, other than that he felt like he'd been run over by a car.

Kate had already seen the obvious trauma to his head; the angry swelling and the egg-sized lump above his temple told her enough. An inch lower and he would probably be dead, she thought, but decided not to impart that small bit of important information. The ribs were also evident in that the bruising was livid – not as significant as Mitch's chest, but still painful – and she guessed that it was nothing more serious than one or two cracked ribs at worst. She was sure a big tough guy like Dan could handle that as well as the thirty or so tiny pellets of shot she had removed from his backside.

He hadn't realised the handful of deep cuts on his wrists where he had clumsily cut his own bindings with a reversed knife; speed and freedom had been more important than accuracy at that point. Kate had bound them tight, but seeing some blood seeping through the dressings made her worry that some sutures would be required.

She relayed this to him, seeing the surprise on his face as he tried to recall how he had cut himself, and said that she needed to check them. Peeling away the bandages, she found that the cuts weren't as severe as she feared, and in consultation with Sera decided to use steri-strips to bind the flesh together in place of sutures and apply new dressings. His main bag of kit was found among the heap and he dressed in his own clothes with difficulty. He then settled himself down next to Mitch. Battered and currently of little use, both of them still had weapons within arm's reach.

The two warriors were propped up in relative comfort and brought hot food. Mitch didn't know how to tell Dan what had brought them to this place, and he seemed so confused that he wasn't sure he should even be told yet.

Being proved wrong moments later, Dan spoke quietly to him.

"Who shot you?" he asked.

"Don't know," Mitch answered after a sigh. "I assume it was catwoman and her mates."

"Tell me," Dan urged him, trying to hide the concern in his voice.

Mitch raised his eyes skyward and answered in the only way he felt truly comfortable. In succinct sentences, he gave Dan the action report without emotion or speculation.

"I was on stag," he said, meaning he was acting as sentry, "and took one to the chest. Heavy calibre but not enough to penetrate the vest. It put me down hard. Everyone tried to get on board the truck but we got attacked from the rear. They came swarming out of the woods and we were close to being overwhelmed." He swallowed and paused to take a sip of his drink before continuing. "Henry broke cover and tried to give them fire and Jack went to drag him back. He took two low in the back. One through-and-through, another lodged inside. He bled out over there," Mitch pointed towards the dark patch on the ground, "because we'd lost most of the medical gear when we ran. We stopped here and Leah went out to raid a hospital for supplies, but Jack passed just after she had left. She was gutted when she got back and took it out on the kid," Mitch said, meaning Henry.

Dan sat in stony-faced silence as he listened to how his group were attacked and had to flee because he wasn't there to protect them.

"We would have been at the ERV yesterday, but the truck was knackered. Neil grafted all day and fixed it, but by then I guess you'd already made new friends," Mitch said to Dan, making him issue an involuntary but agonising laugh.

"Yeah," Dan replied when the pain had subsided. "I saw the truck missing from the gateway but had one of them chase me on a bike. One of our bikes. I put some distance in but they came after me in my own bloody motor. I tell you what, seeing that Foxhound in your wing mirror is intimidating. I outpaced it, but the bike stayed with me…"

"Did you kill any?" Mitch asked out of a genuine want to know if any of them suffered.

"Not sure, but the biker went under the back wheel, so if he's not dead, I doubt he's having a good day," Dan answered with a cruel smirk which pleased Mitch no end. "After that, I waited at the bridge for two days and was about to make plans to move on until they came for me. Front and back. Dropped one at distance but then I got taken out. Fucker nearly beheaded me with an axe!" he said, as though the audacity of such behaviour was unheard of. "Woke up and met some twat who calls himself 'the hunter', so I popped his nose and slotted a few more of them before Leah saved my ass."

"Again!" they chorused, prompting more laughter and the subsequent wincing in pain.

"Your gear?" Mitch asked when the cursing had subsided.

"Lost the Land Rover, my go-bag, a slab of 5.56, and my M4 was pretty much bent in half courtesy of the axe," he answered sadly.

The two sat in silence for a while until Dan peeled the cellophane off a new packet of cigarettes and lit one.

"Oh shit," Mitch said with a start. "I completely forgot! What about the radio message?"

Eyes wide, Dan too realised he had completely failed to recollect the reason they were separated in the first place.

"Leah!" he yelled, regretting it instantly as his ribs went into spasm.

"What?" came the sarcastic-sounding reply from ground level a moment later.

"Fetch me a map showing the south coast and get the others. You're going to want to hear this," he said, suddenly alive with renewed energy.

NOT SOMEONE YOU WANT TO MESS WITH

Panting from the effort, Lexi bent down with her hands on her knees and breathed hard as her rifle dangled on its sling. The bloodied knife was still in her right hand, and as she watched a thick globule of blood gather and drip from the sharp point of the blade, she marvelled that she felt nothing. No appalling sense of morality, no guilt like when she had killed her first person all that time ago from the roof of a disused building.

She had killed, Paul had killed, even Chris had shot two of the attackers, although the spaced-out look on his face made her feel sure that he was going to throw up at any point.

Looking over at the last member of their group, she watched in awe as he stalked the remaining survivor of the attack on them; a thin young man was dragging himself away with part of his leg in ruin from a blast of Simon's shotgun. Crying with fear and pain, he squealed like a piglet lifted from the teat when he felt the big boot land high on his back to pin him to the ground.

Lexi's head tilted to the side as she wondered what Simon was doing, then that look of curiosity turned to abject horror as she witnessed the big man reach down with both hands and take a firm grip under the chin of his victim. With a savage grunt, he wrenched the head upwards, instantly stifling the cry of anguish and terror, and was rewarded with a sickening series of sinewy popping noises as the spinal cord was snapped back and the delicate conjoining of the upper spine was mangled into unrecognisable ruin.

Turning back towards the others, Lexi saw a flash of the inner monster Simon had just become, and just as her hand began to flutter towards the grip of her gun to raise it in instinctive fear, the look dissolved and his passive and reassuring face was displayed there instead. Lexi looked at him in shock, unable to tear her eyes away from the horror of what she had just witnessed their passive companion do to another person.

True, they had all just killed, but she was worried that Simon had enjoyed it. Just before her mouth began to move and say something which she wasn't even sure of yet, his self-effacing smile returned and disarmed her instantly.

"I'll make a start on those wheels, shall I?" he said, striding off towards the Land Rover without waiting for a response.

Reloading his weapon, Paul walked up to his partner and misread her look of utter horror.

"Are you OK?" he asked, concern evident in his words. "Are you hurt?"

"What? No," she replied, shaking herself out of her stupor and questioning if she had really seen what had just happened. "No, I'm fine," she said, gaining control of herself. "It's just Simon…"

"Is he hurt?" Paul asked with worry.

"No," said Lexi again, pausing and gathering her thoughts, "he's not hurt, but I did just see him snap a man's neck like it was dinner."

Paul didn't understand her fully. How could he? The look on Simon's face wasn't something anyone could accurately describe.

"Good lad!" Paul said cheerfully, before walking towards the Land Rover and gently taking the gun from Chris's shaking hands.

Lexi stood alone and surveyed the carnage around her. She was certain at the time that counterattack was the best option for survival, and her assertion was made true by the eight dead bodies around them, which was all that remained of the failed ambush. Thoughts crowded in her head, bumping off one another like dodgems and not allowing any of it to connect and make sense. She couldn't understand why a group of people had attacked them with weapons more suited to cavemen than new-world survivors, but mostly she couldn't understand how anyone could enjoy killing.

Unable to articulate her thoughts just yet, she returned to the truck to keep watch while the two ruined wheels were discarded and sixty per cent of their spares were used to get them underway again. And she watched Simon like a hawk.

ONWARDS TO SANCTUARY

Dan told them about the message he had heard. He told them, from what he could remember as his notepad had been taken from him when he was captured, what the words meant and what he had found on the map. He showed them now as everyone lined up to pass him and look at where he held the tip of his knife on the small bay on the south coast of the continent. He told them that the place was where they should go to try and seek help in getting themselves patched up and over the water towards their eventual goal of Africa.

The group buzzed with excitement. A welcome excitement after the traumatic events of the last few days which left them cramped in a single vehicle with limited supplies. It had left two of them badly hurt and one of them dead. It had left them all feeling hopeless, scared and lost. Now they had renewed energy, a sense of purpose and an achievable goal instead of an open-ended trek into dwindling hope.

Although still in a bad way as a whole, the group readied themselves and set off the following morning with a bearing of southwest and taking the long way around to avoid crossing the wide ravine via the ill-fated bridge. Before they left, Dan insisted that he get to see Jack's final resting place. Leaning down stiffly under constant threat of falling over thanks to the concussion wreaking havoc with his equilibrium, he rested a flat hand on the crude wooden cross which marked the grave.

Standing up straight again and looking down, he uttered a few words before he turned away. "Blessings of God to you, friend."

After forty-eight hours, their fuel supply began to run low. They had used up all of the diesel from the jerrycans they had packed as an emergency reserve, and Dan silently blamed himself for losing his vehicle and the fifty or so litres of go-juice he had on board.

They were reduced to siphoning what Neil jokingly referred to as "liquid dinosaurs" from decaying cars and having to add a small dose of ethanol acquired by Neil at the garage to keep the engine running on the poor-quality fuel. They could not take the risk of shutting down the engine for fear it wouldn't restart, so the few able drivers took it in turns to take the wheel and make slow progress so as not to put the truck under any undue pressure.

Dan hated the journey: not that he couldn't stand the discomfort he was in, but because he was unable to help run the show. That honour and responsibility fell to both Leah and Neil, as neither Dan nor Mitch were of any use. To know that he was more of a hindrance than a help crucified him, and he had to force himself to take a metaphorical step back and allow the people he trusted most to do what he knew they could do.

Despite the very close proximity, he was happy that he didn't once see Henry's face looking at him; the boy was probably too scared or ashamed to make eye contact even though Dan felt that Leah had already punished him as much as was needed. His own conscience would do the rest.

Nestled among the bags in the back of the truck, he found that he actually enjoyed the time spent cuddled up to Marie and Ash, despite the painfully uncomfortable ride.

Enjoyment was probably a strong description for what he felt overall, but he found himself thinking that he might even like taking a day off in the future. Either way, the sense of semi-enjoyment he felt was shattered when the engine stalled and the truck ground to a juddering halt.

Neil climbed down from behind the wheel, walked to the front of the lifeless engine, and just stared at the dirty green metal. His face showed a twitch, quickly brought under control, until the involuntary movement returned with more force and his face contorted as though possessed.

Quite without warning, Neil began to kick the front of the dead truck and swear at it foully. Very rarely had even Dan seen his friend's temper, and to most, it came as a complete shock to see the ever-smiling and painfully comedic man utterly lose his shit in a nuclear way.

Unfortunately for Neil, his slight lack of coordination combined with his overwhelming anger made for more inadvertent humour when he overstretched a kick aimed at the grille and fell hard on his backside. Getting to his feet with as much dignity as he could muster, he dusted himself down and addressed the small crowd gathered in embarrassed silence.

"I don't suppose," he said in his favourite accent, "that any of you are in possession of one diesel fuel filter to fit a Perkins engine?"

One or two slow shakes of the head disturbed the group's stillness, having mistakenly taken the question as anything more than comical rhetoric to disguise his loss of control.

"Well, chaps," announced Neil, "we seem to be buggered then!"

A small ripple of laughter ran through them as their nerves got the better of them in the fraught situation. Dan watched on, leaning lightly on Marie's shoulder, as he still suffered from bouts of dizziness, and glanced around looking for Leah. Catching sight of her a short distance away, she was already spreading the map out on the roadway. Walking over to her, carefully placing one foot down at a time, as he still didn't trust his ability to stay upright, he saw the girl working hard to try and figure out where they were.

"Need any help, kid?" Dan asked her, only to close his mouth when she held her forefinger aloft. The finger was meant to convey a polite request for him not to interrupt her thought process or she would have to start again. Feeling no sense of anger at being told so rudely to can it, he waited patiently until the finger was lowered and she turned to look at him.

Only then did he see the red rings around her eyes. The girl had barely slept for more than a few hours a day over the last God knows how long, and even though her mind was alert, her body was showing signs it was beginning to fail.

"There should be buildings about four Ks ahead," she said, following her assessment up with a hopeful, "I think." Gathering herself, she looked him straight in the eye and issued her instructions. "You stay here, Adam can keep watch. I'll take Ash and Jimmy ahead to see what we can find. There's very little chance we'll see anyone here because this is the middle of bloody nowhere, but let's not get complacent, shall we?"

A couple of years ago, receiving orders from a teenager festooned with weaponry would have seemed odd to say the least. Instead, Dan nodded his agreement but felt compelled to add his own words of warning.

"Fine. Be back by nightfall or I'm coming after you myself," he told her.

Fighting back her urge to inform Dan that he couldn't fight his way clear of a paper bag at that point, she nodded in agreement and turned away. Dan's further instructions drifted over her shoulder as she walked.

"And when you're back, you need to sleep," he said, inviting no recourse for argument.

Turning as she walked to pace backwards, Leah displayed her biggest fake grin and raised two thumbs up to him.

Cheeky cow, he thought to himself with a smirk. As he watched her go, his right leg twitched and threatened to buckle under his weight. Turning to Marie, he expressed his opinion that sitting down in the very immediate future would be beneficial to his health. He didn't make the refuge of the back of the truck; instead, he stumbled just before and, unfortunately for him, in direct sight of Kate.

He was unsure which hurt more: the throbbing pain in his head combined with the agonising soreness of his neck or the berating he received for being on his feet.

"I swear," complained Kate, "your bloody head injuries will be the death of me!"

"I rather suspect they're more likely to be the death of me," he answered with slurring sarcasm.

Leah and Jimmy went forwards at a comfortable trot with Ash keeping pace effortlessly beside them. Rounding a left-hand bend as they went downhill, they saw a dozen or so buildings nestled in the small gulley ahead. Stopping at a distance and carefully surveying the scene below, Leah was happy that she saw no movement and no sign of recent activity. Glancing up at the sky, she told Jimmy they had maybe three hours to search the place for vehicles before they had to be setting off back to the others.

Saying nothing in response, Jimmy merely hefted his faithful crowbar and gave her a tired smile of agreement.

"Let's do this," she said.

OH, HOW THE MIGHTY HAVE FALLEN

A week prior, she had been riding in a bombproof military scout truck at the head of a four-vehicle convoy, been carrying enough spare ammunition to turn the tide of a major conflict, and held supplies to keep them fed and fuelled for months.

Now, almost ashamed more than embarrassed, she was sitting in the front seat of a nine-year-old seven-seat people carrier and towing a rickety trailer which was packed to the point of overflowing with their kit and remaining stores. The only other form of viable transport found in the tiny village was in the form of pedal cycles, of which six of their group now followed on behind her while others were forced to walk. At their desperately slow rate of progress, it took them most of the following day to source a further vehicle sufficiently preserved in a dusty barn to get started.

Neil impressed them all by pouring lighter fluid on the air intake and telling them all to step back as the engine fired into life and revved violently until it settled down. Now, packed in more tightly than they had been in a single army truck, the two overloaded vehicles wound their ponderous way towards the coast at horribly low speeds due to the combination of gradient and weight.

Calling a stop to their travels for the day, she watched as the others unfolded themselves from the musty cabins and spilled into the fresh air. Clearing a small cafe for the night, Leah emerged to announce the area clear.

By this point, people had abandoned all hope of comfort and simply threw down their sleeping bags where they believed enough space existed for them to lie down. Within minutes, the dusty floor was a mess of snoring, multicoloured maggots of human proportions.

Wiping two glasses on the arm of her long-sleeved black top, she poured a couple of measures from a bottle she had found behind the counter. Tipping back one of the chairs on the small terrace outside, she sat next to Dan and handed him a glass.

Sniffing it with some trepidation, Dan sipped the drink to find it to be some fruity distilled substance, similar to the Calvados of the northern parts of the country but sweeter. Amused at Leah's grimace as she sipped from her own glass, he watched as she leaned back to relax.

"One more day to the coast," she said to him in quiet estimation.

"One more day," he agreed, sipping again and fearing that he might actually develop a taste for whatever it was he was drinking.

"Then what?" she asked him.

Lighting a cigarette to fill the pause he needed to phrase his answer, he leaned back his own chair like hers and blew out a stream of smoke.

"Then we hope they are actually friendly and can help us," he said, before adding seriously, "but if they aren't, I need you on top form to kick some ass." With that, he leaned over and took the glass from her unresisting hand. "So get some sleep."

Sitting alone as he smoked, he drained first his own and then Leah's glass as he mulled over the options they might face the following evening.

THE HUNT

"Calling all survivors. We offer security, food and family. Our city has stood for generations. We are strong. We live and offer life. We are Sanctuary. Fort of the south sea," he told his assembled men in French, reading from the notepad in his hand.

After the gall of this Englishman had reduced his number to a mere thirty-eight, he had vowed to exact a brutal and slow revenge on him. Him and the others who had come for him in the big green truck which his scouts had reported was last seen fleeing to the north.

"So," he said, arms wide and a wicked smile showing on his face under the livid bruising of his recently ruined nose, "who is hungry for seafood and revenge?"

As one, his small army roared their approval of his plan. In truth, they would have followed him anywhere, though most were growing bored of their nomadic existence as they roamed the country in search of plunder. Each and every one of them had served with him in Africa, and a good number of his best fighters were former Foreign Legion.

Now they would chase this man to the edge of the sea.

The hunt was on.

SANCTUARY

Exhausted, cramped and longing for the freedom to sit without having to be in contact with so many others in a confined space, Leah happily exited the car and stretched her back.

Walking slowly forwards with her arms out to her sides, she glanced skywards to her left and marvelled at the impossibly steep slopes and impregnable walls. Pacing intently towards the lowered portcullis in the only break in the ancient wall that she could see, a light shone down through the early evening gloom and fixed her on the spot.

Hearing no challenge issued, but mindful of Dan's advice, she stayed where she was and waited.

And waited.

A single line of French was shouted at her with an inflection which suggested it was a question.

"Do you speak English?" she shouted back.

A pause filled the air until the response came. "A little. What do you want?"

Her relief was palpable. Clearing her throat and holding her head high, she shouted back that she was with the group of survivors in the cars behind her. That they meant no harm and had heard the radio message offering safety. That they had been attacked numerous times since they left England on their journey, and that they were begging for help from the people of Sanctuary.

Only silence answered her impassioned plea, and just as her heart began to sink as she thought they would be turned away, a creaking noise announced the raising of the gate.

They were greeted with kindness, and as Dan kept a hand on the shoulders of both Marie and Leah to steady his dizziness, he stared in awe at the high fortress protecting the gate in the wall which extended around the entire area between two steep cliffs. As he passed through the ancient but still formidable gateway, he looked skywards once more to find that the fortress built into the cliff was actually separate from the walled town and effectively prevented anyone from gaining a position to be able to attack the entrance to the enclosure.

In the sinking sunlight, he could make out a high watchtower at each end of the protected bay and a cluster of houses which extended beyond the huge central keep behind the gateway and down to the water's edge.

The radio message wasn't exaggerating, he told himself. This place really was impregnable: he'd need air superiority, a small navy and modern explosives or artillery to take this place.

His light-headedness wasn't only caused by the concussion he had suffered; it was due in part to the relief he felt at being in a place where the outside world could be shut away and he could finally sleep soundly without his boots on and without his guns ready.

The place truly was an impregnable sanctuary.

EPILOGUE

They had been fed. They had experienced their first hot showers in months and could hardly believe that Sanctuary boasted not only the most secure defences they had ever seen but also had power courtesy of, they were told, the two massive wind turbines on the mountain top. If they looked closely, they could see the automated flashing red lights that served as a warning to the aircraft which were unlikely to ever fly close to the spinning blades again.

Dan had shaved with hot water and a fresh razor. They were asked politely to secure all of their weapons in a locked room as they entered the keep, and the presence of four armed and nervous-looking men had ensured their compliance. Almost. Dan kept hold of the suppressed Walther, which he stored under the pillow in the comfortable room he and Marie had been given in the big central keep, and he still had a knife in his waistband. Marie's joy and relief at sleeping on a real mattress weren't due to her being spoilt or precious; her pregnancy was advancing to the point where she felt uncomfortable most of the time and the prospect of a real bed was heaven on earth to her.

"Hey!" she said, grabbing Dan's attention. "Remember when I asked when we were going to catch a break?" she asked with a rueful smile.

"I think we just have," he answered, smiling back at her with all the unfamiliarity of his freshly shaved face.

Telling the dog to stay and not to climb on the bed, he left with Marie to answer the summons to meet the leadership of the town. As he closed the door, he was certain he heard the small sound of Ash leaping onto the duvet to get comfortable.

Dan, Marie and Leah stood in what had been the great hall where the medieval rulers of old once passed judgement, and waited in silence for the welcome speech.

A tall, thin woman entered the room. She bore a wide smile and shook hands with all of them in turn, introducing herself in accented English as Polly.

"You're American?" Leah asked, unsure at her curious accent.

"I'm Quebecois," she answered patiently, bordering on the condescending, as she hadn't yet fully understood the teenager's status in their group. "French Canadian," she explained, as though that made everything fall into place.

Polly began to embark on a great description of what they had achieved there since the fall of humanity as she described it, but Dan's attention was snatched away by Marie's gasp.

Fearing that she was in pain, he turned to her and opened his mouth to ask if she was OK until he too heard the source of her shock.

From behind a door off the main hall came the unmistakable sound of a baby crying.

The story continues in AFTER IT HAPPENED BOOK 6:
REBELLION

COMING SOON!

A message from the author

Thanks for reading. Please leave a review on Amazon if you enjoyed it!

You can find me on:

Facebook: Devon C Ford

Twitter: @DevonFordAuthor

Subscribe to my email list and read my blog:

www.devonfordauthor.uk

Printed in Great Britain
by Amazon